Where the Creeks Meet

Other books by Lael Littke

Books for Children and Young People:
Wilmer the Watchdog (Western, 1969)

Tell Me When I Can Go (Scholastic, 1978)

Cave-in! (Children's Press, 1981)

Trish for President (Harcourt Brace Jovanovich, 1984)

Shanny on Her Own (Harcourt Brace Jovanovich, 1985)

Loydene in Love (Harcourt Brace Jovanovich, 1986)

Where the Creeks Meet

Lael Littke

Deseret Book Company
Salt Lake City, Utah

©1987 Lael Littke

All rights reserved. No part of this book may be reproduced
in any form or by any means without permission in writing
from the publisher, Deseret Book Company, P.O. Box 30178,
Salt Lake City, Utah 84130.

Deseret Book is a registered trademark of Deseret Book Company.

First printing in paperbound edition, August 1989

Library of Congress Cataloging-in-Publication Data

Littke, Lael.
    Where the creeks meet.

    Summary: A reluctant newcomer to a small Idaho town,
teenage Ashley longs to return to California but her
increasing involvement with a mysterious young man who
claims to be a ghost helps her see herself, her family,
and her friends in a different way.
    [1. Moving, Household—Fiction.   2. Emotional problems
—Fiction.   3. Conduct of life—Fiction.   4. Mystery and
detective stories]   I. Title.
PZ7.L719Wh   1987   [Fic]   87-15592
ISBN 0-87579-092-5 (hardbound ed.)
ISBN 0-87579-229-4 (paperbound ed.)

Printed in the United States of America
10   9   8   7   6   5   4   3   2   1

To Juanita, in memoriam

Chapter One

Gideon told me right at the first that he had secrets. I thought he was talking about having dandruff, or something like that. How could I guess what his secrets really were? My sixteen years had been pleasant, spent mostly around California swimming pools. If a thought about anything besides my own comfort ever entered my head, it hurried out before it could do any damage.

I wish I could rewind time and make a lot of things unhappen.

But how far back would I have to go to change things for Gideon?

It was my parents' idea to move our family to Blue Creek. I didn't want to go. But I went.

The main thing I noticed about driving from California to Idaho was the way the highways narrowed. We started out on the freeway, eight lanes wide back home in Pasadena. Somewhere along the way it squeezed down to four lanes. In northern Utah we left Interstate 15 and followed two-lane U.S. 91. When we got to Idaho, we branched off onto a narrow country road that led to Blue Creek.

It was like heading into a funnel, the boundaries of my life narrowing with each mile we drove.

"Before we get to our new house, we'll be driving on an unpaved dirt road," Dad said.

I groaned. "It sounds like *Little House on the Prairie*."

"You'll love it," Dad said.

"*I'll* love it," Finn said, and Truman seconded the motion with a "Me, too."

Finn was nine and Truman, six. What did they know?

Mom half-turned in her seat and smiled back at me. "Give it a chance, Ashley. That's all we ask."

I didn't say anything. What chance could I give it? Who needed narrow green valleys and orange cows and creeks that glitter in the sunlight like cheap glass rings?

"You have to admit it's pretty here," Dad said.

Big deal. What good was pretty if it replaced familiar and fun and friends? Who could even think about pretty when I had left my best friend, Valerie, back in Pasadena, and even worse, Richard. Richard and that spiffy little red truck he'd gotten for his seventeenth birthday. Richard, who wore T-shirts with the sleeves cut off, and a rabbit's foot dangling from a belt loop of his jeans.

Every girl in school had envied me because of Richard.

"So how long do you think it will take Richard to find somebody new?"

I didn't realize I'd spoken aloud until Mom said, "You're better off without Richard, Ashley. He isn't the kind of boy you want to run around with. One of these days he's going to pile himself up, one way or another, and I'm glad you're not there to pile up with him."

"It's my life," I whispered. It was an old argument.

Mom sighed.

"Are we almost there?" Truman asked. He'd asked that question on an average of three times per hour for the past two days. "How much farther is it to Blue Creek?"

"Just another inch." Finn held up his map for Truman to see, pointing to a speck down in the southeast corner of Idaho. Finn is the World's Foremost Authority. He'll tell you about anything. You don't even have to ask.

Truman squinted at the map. "Is that Blue Creek? It looks like a period."

"That's exactly what it is," I said. "A period. The end."

This time Mom turned around so she could look directly at me. "Honey, could you just wait until you see it before you turn off on it? Your father and I feel very good about this move."

For Mom's benefit I nodded. "I'll give it a try." But I still felt I hadn't really been given any say about it. Oh, we'd had a council about it in family home evening, of course. Everybody had a vote. But it was rigged right from the start. Finn has a Tom Sawyer complex. Dad mentioned a creek in the front yard and a canyon in back, and Finn packed his suitcase. Mom talked about tobogganing on our own hills in the winter, and Truman asked how soon we could leave.

They spoke horses to me, but it didn't work. There'd been a time when I would have sold my brothers for a horse. But I grew out of that, just as I grew out of my Roving Rangers Day Camp T-shirt.

Gloomily I looked out at the willow-shaded creek that ran alongside the road. There were mountains in the background, but they weren't as high as the San Gabriels back in Pasadena. They were rounded and kind of fuzzy with what Dad said was sagebrush. He'd told us there was a mountain named George on our property. I thought of writing a letter to Valerie, saying, "I have a new friend. His name is George Hill. He's a mountain of a guy."

I wondered if Val would figure that one out. She'd

probably think I was running around with a wrestler. She'd probably let it slip to Richard, and that would be the last I'd hear from him.

I sighed loudly.

Dad was leaning out of the car window, sniffing. "There's nothing as nice as the smell of new-mown hay."

That made Finn and Truman lean out of their window and snuffle like a couple of dumb dogs.

Dad grew up on a farm in Idaho somewhere, and he was always talking about how terrific his boyhood was. He's a dentist now, and his practice wasn't doing too well in California. When he heard that Prentiss, which is the nearest town to Blue Creek, needed a dentist, he flew up to check it out. Then he took Mom up there and they found this farm that was for sale in Blue Creek. They decided we'd live in Blue Creek and Dad would drive to Prentiss to do his dentist thing.

Mom is a city girl, but she likes to bake bread and grow gardens and that kind of thing. She was a school counselor in Pasadena, and it surprised me that she'd want to chuck everything to move to the sticks. But she couldn't wait to get there.

We were passing a sign that read "Blue Creek, Pop. 207."

With us moving in, they could change that to Pop. 212. But they might as well wait a little while, I thought, because I intended to head back to California—and Richard—as soon as possible. It was my life. What I did with it was my business, and if I messed up, it wasn't going to hurt anybody but me. Why couldn't Mom and Dad accept that?

"We're going to stop at the general store," Dad said, pointing up ahead to a white painted wooden building on a hillside overlooking the valley. "It's really something."

It was something, all right. Talk about *Little House on the Prairie!* That general store could have been lifted right off the Hollywood set for the show.

We parked in front of the big glass windows over which was a sign that read "Blue Creek Merc. Kendall Atwood, Prop."

"Mercantile," the World's Foremost Authority explained, though no one had asked. "That's what M-e-r-c means. Kendall Atwood, Proprietor."

"Thanks," I said. "I don't know what I would have done without that information."

The inside of the store was more than ever like a movie set. There was even a potbelly stove in one corner of the big room. Shelves along the side walls and down the middle of the room held canned goods and bolts of cloth and eggs and cooking pots made of thick, black iron. All the stuff you'd expect to see in a country store back in 1890. I found myself wondering if we'd got caught in some kind of time warp.

But then I saw a bunch of pocket calculators in a glass counter that also held candy. There was a guy about my age looking at those calculators. I glanced at him just as he looked my way. He scowled a little, then looked back at the calculators.

He had dark red hair and blue eyes and would rate a 10 on anybody's chart. I might have been interested, if I hadn't been in love with Richard.

Just then Kendall Atwood, Prop., spoke to him. "Find the one you want, Whit?"

Whit. Short for what? Whitney, maybe?

"I need one for my calculus class next fall," Whit said. "One that has sine and cosine functions and logarithms and all that."

"Got just the one for you, son." Mr. Atwood moved over to the glass case and opened it.

I wondered if Whit was from somewhere else, too. I mean, the guys from a place like Blue Creek would be studying agriculture and animal husbandry and things like that, wouldn't they?

Mom paid for the things she'd gathered up in a basket. Crackers from a barrel over by the potbelly stove. Oranges wrapped in red tissue paper. A blue-flowered potholder. Things with a down-homey look. Things we didn't need.

"Come *on*, Ashley." Finn joggled my arm. "We're leaving. I can't wait to get to our new house."

You could almost see the Tom Sawyer freckles pop out on his face. He pulled me outside before I could make a decision to talk to Whit, to see if he might be from California too. I didn't even get to see if he bought the calculator.

We all got back into the car and headed up a narrow valley.

Dad wasn't kidding about the dirt road. The main highway was only two lanes, but the road we turned off on was hardly wide enough for one car. We bounced along over rocks and ruts, and my spirits fell even lower. If Mom and Dad had brought us up there *before* we sold our California house, I would have refused to move. But they had made the trip to Idaho while Finn and Truman and I were still in school. They said we should trust the wisdom of their decision.

Willows and other bushes hung over the car, almost touching the roof. It was like driving through a dark tunnel. A hillside rose sharply on the right side of the road and the creek was to the left, making my funneled feeling even stronger.

Then I saw the guy. At first I thought it was Whit. But

Whit had been dressed in tan pants and a green T-shirt, just like any California guy. This one wore dark, wide-legged pants, a short jacket, and a cap with a bill.

He stood on the other side of the creek, with his hand on a tree. He didn't try to hide or anything, but he looked ready to run.

"I wonder who that is," I said.

"Where?" Finn craned his neck. "I didn't see anybody."

I pointed. "There."

Mom and Truman turned their heads and even Dad sneaked a fast look.

"Are you sure there was someone there?" he said. "This is *our* land."

"He was there, all right," I said.

That was the first time I saw Gideon. Gideon, the good. Gideon, the grave. Gideon, who changed my life.

Chapter Two

I had this fantasy all the way from California that Mom and Dad would hate the house when they saw it again. I played the scene over and over in my head. Mom would sit bolt upright and say, "Oh, Bill, I didn't remember that it looked so dreadful." Dad would say, "You're right, Marge. We can't possibly ask our kids to live in a place like that."

Then, without even getting out of the car, we would turn around and head back home to California.

Mom sat bolt upright when we turned off the rutty road and crossed the stone bridge over the creek, but she got her lines all wrong. What she said was, "Oh, Bill, it's heaven!"

"Heaven" was a white house with red trim. It fit into the hillside behind it like a person resting in a comfortable easy chair.

A man came out of the big red barn nearby while we were unloading our suitcases from the car. I had seen the barn as we drove across the stone bridge and I wondered about horses. But I didn't want to say anything, or Mom and Dad would think I'd been converted to this place.

"This is Mr. Morehead," Dad said, shaking hands with the man, who said, "Call me Abel."

If he'd been dressed in a business suit rather than blue overalls, I'd have guessed that Abel was a college professor. He was tall and skinny, and he had hair the color of the gray enamel pot Mom used to cook oatmeal.

"Abel's going to be taking care of the place while I'm in town fixing teeth," Dad said. "He owns the next farm down the creek."

"The wife did dinner for you," Abel said. "It's in the kitchen. Just spaghetti and meatballs."

Finn and Truman, thinking only of their stomachs as usual, headed for the house. I didn't think I'd get any help from them in moving our family back home. And Mom was practically glassy-eyed over having such thoughtful, friendly neighbors. I sighed and went upstairs to inspect my new room and write a letter to Richard.

It wasn't until much later, when I was getting ready for bed, that I thought again of the guy I'd seen among the trees by the creek. I wondered if he was still there. I looked out of my window at the night, lit only by the stars. No street lamps. No cars going by. Just darkness.

Was the guy out there now, watching me standing at the window?

Yanking down the blind, I switched off the light. I spread my sleeping bag on the floor and crawled into it.

The moving van arrived the next day with our things from home. Mom found just the right place for everything. When she finished arranging it all, our familiar things looked as if they had always been there in those unfamiliar rooms.

I was the only thing that didn't belong.

During the next couple of days Finn and Truman began building a dam in the creek. Mom started to plant a garden in the space Abel had already plowed. Dad went to Prentiss to do what dentists do.

I moped around, thinking that if I made myself obnoxious enough with my sighing and eye-rolling, Mom and Dad would send me back home just to maintain their sanity.

Abel Morehead tried to get me to ride some of the horses in the green pasture behind the barn. One day, out of desperation for something to do, I told him I was ready.

"Ever ride much?" Abel asked. He was hitching a couple of horses to an old farm wagon. He said he preferred that to a truck for puttering around the place.

"I've ridden a lot," I said. That wasn't completely untrue. We spent a lot of time on horses when I went to the Roving Rangers Day Camp. The only difference between riding those horses and riding a tree trunk was that maybe the tree trunk moved faster.

Abel looked at me a little skeptically, I thought. "Skyrocket. He's the one for you. You can try some of the others later this summer."

I climbed up on the bottom rail of the corral fence and looked at the horses. "Maybe I won't be here that long."

"Oh?" Abel sounded mildly curious. "Where you going?"

"Back to California. I'm here just temporarily."

He squinted at me. "Got a boyfriend there?"

"Yes." I stepped down from the rail and smiled at Abel. "Richard. He's my guy."

"Nice feller?"

"My folks don't think so," I said. "But he's terrific. He can dance up a storm. You should see him handle a motorcycle. And he drives that little red truck of his like a racer. He's into guns, too. Even taught *me* to shoot." I didn't say that I didn't like the guns. I hadn't even told Richard that.

Abel nodded. "Sounds dangerous."

"Maybe that's why I love him. It's always exciting, being with Richard. We might get married when I get back." Well, that wasn't too far from wrong. Richard had said he'd even marry me to keep me with him. I didn't know if he was kidding or not. But I knew my parents would never give me permission. So I let them take me away.

"Little young, aren't you?"

"It's the only way I can be sure of staying there." I wondered if I'd said too much. "Abel, I'd appreciate it if you didn't say anything to my folks about this yet."

"I don't tell secrets," Abel said. "I'll go get Skyrocket for you."

He brought the tall bay horse and saddled him. "Need a hoist on?"

I shook my head and swung up onto Skyrocket. "Thanks. Now where's a good place to go?"

Abel waved an arm. "Anywhere. Nice view from the top of George Hill. You can see the river."

"Funny name for a mountain," I said.

"Named after a feller who used to live up there where the creeks meet. George Glessing."

That surprised me. "I thought ours was the last house in this end of the valley."

Abel gazed off toward George Hill. "Not much of the old house left anymore." He scratched at his chin. "Wouldn't go there if I was you. Boggy. Horse could get swamped in."

Mom came out of the house just then.

"Ashley," she called, "if you're riding somewhere, could you go to the general store and pick up some vinegar and paper towels?"

"Sure," I called back. "Well, Skyrocket, let's go."

I said good-bye to Abel and we blasted off. By the time we got to the main road, Skyrocket had worked himself up to a casual saunter.

Oh, Richard, I whispered, *where are you when I need you?*

Mom and Dad might want to live life at a slower pace, but I was going to die if something didn't speed up a little — and soon.

At the general store I picked up some chocolate-covered peanuts and a can of 7-Up along with Mom's vinegar and paper towels. It would be almost worth the trip to break loose from the healthy diet Mom was keeping us on.

I carried my purchases over to the counter, where Kendall Atwood, Prop., was busy with another customer. Standing by the calculator case, I thought about the guy named Whit who'd been there the day we arrived.

There was a girl about my age a few feet from me. She held a baby on one blue-jeaned hip and kept an eye on another little kid who must have been about three.

She smiled at me. "Hi. You must be Ashley Lassiter."

My mouth dropped open. "How did you know?"

"No secrets in a country town," she said. "We all know your family moved onto the old Eskelsen place."

"That's more than I knew," I told her. "I didn't know it was the old Eskelsen place."

The girl laughed. "It will *always* be the old Eskelsen place, even if you live there for the next thirty years. The Johnsons, who lived there before you, moved in before I was born, but it was still called the old Eskelsen place all the years they lived there." The baby on her hip whimpered and she jiggled him a little. "People here don't take to change."

I wondered what I could say to this girl. The thoughts of living there on "the old Eskelsen place" for thirty years kind of wiped me out.

Finally I said, "Cute baby you've got there."

The girl kissed the top of the baby's head. "Yeah, Fuffer is a cute little snuggle-bunny, all right." She looked around for the other kid, who was upending brooms in the corner. "Petey John, you put those right back like they were," she commanded.

Petey John went right on upending more brooms.

I cleared my throat. "You know my name, but I guess I don't know yours."

"Oh, sorry," the girl said. "This year I'm Racine Wisconsin."

"Racine Wisconsin?" I was bewildered.

"Last year I was Spring Breeze," Racine Wisconsin said. "Actually, my name is LeeAnne McFadden. But that doesn't make a statement, if you know what I mean. So I'm trying on another name."

She reminded me of a lady I knew back home who married a man whose last name was Young, so she changed her first name from Edna to Eternally.

Racine was still talking. "It's sort of like trying on dresses, you know? Eventually I'll find the one that will be *me*."

"I never thought of doing that," I said in admiration.

"You don't need to," Racine said. "Your name says a lot already." She closed her eyes and tipped her head back. "Ashley Lassiter," she whispered.

The way she said it made me think of a summer wind blowing out of Eaton Canyon back home in Pasadena.

I told Racine what I was thinking.

"See?" she said. "Your name says you're warm and good and you know where you're coming from."

I liked Racine Wisconsin. I guess she liked me too, because she said, "Why don't you ride your horse over to my house sometime, Ashley? Just turn right instead of left by the old yellow schoolhouse. We live a mile up the road in a tall brick house with lots of kids around it."

I couldn't believe she had *more* children. Maybe she was older than I thought.

"Sure, Racine," I said. "I'd like to come."

It was Racine's turn to be waited on by Kendall Atwood, Prop. When she was finished, she went over to get the other little kid and set all the brooms upright again. Then she waited for me to pay for my stuff and join her. We walked outside together.

"Have you been to the haunted house up there above the old Eskelsen place yet?" she asked.

Coming out of the blue like that, it gave me a little chill. "I didn't even know there *was* a haunted house."

Racine shifted the baby on her hip. "Guess the Johnsons didn't mention it for fear you wouldn't want to buy the place. It's up where the creeks meet."

I wondered why Abel hadn't told me about the house. He had just said the area was boggy.

"You know," I said, "that's the most interesting thing I've heard since I got here."

Racine grinned. "You and I are going to get along fine, Ashley. We'll go up there together someday. It's been a while since I've been there."

Just then a battered blue van drove up. The guy named Whit got out.

"The groceries are inside," Racine said. "Ashley, this

is Whit. Whit, this is Ashley." She nodded her head toward each of us.

Whit scowled as if he didn't like me. "Hi," he said, then headed for the store. "I'll get the groceries, Racine. You put the kids in the car."

I figured he must be her husband and wondered how she could stand such a cranky guy.

"Don't forget," Racine said, hoisting Fuffer and Petey John into the car. "Come and see me soon."

I got back on Skyrocket and we snailed it toward home.

But I didn't go straight home. I decided to ride up around the haunted house, if I could find it. I had to have something to write to Val about. I didn't think I'd mention it to Richard. He didn't like things like that. "Halloween stuff," he'd call it.

The road ended in a tangle of weeds about half a mile from our driveway. Since both Abel and Racine had mentioned "where the creeks meet," I followed the creek, figuring I would know when I was there if I found another creek. It wasn't easy going because the underbrush was heavy, and limbs from the tall trees dropped down to hold us back. But Skyrocket kept plodding on.

I didn't see the house at first. The two creeks were there, one rushing down out of a ravine and the other just sort of meandering across a meadow to my right. They met and became a bigger stream, which I knew flowed down out of the narrow valley to another creek, which in turn probably ran on until it came to the river we had passed on the way to Blue Creek. And the river flowed into other rivers and all of them probably ended up in the Pacific Ocean. Maybe the very water that was flowing past me right at that moment might someday wash the beaches of California where Richard and Valerie and all my other friends were playing volleyball and getting summer tans.

Then I saw it. Or what was left of it. It hadn't been a very big house to begin with. Now it was crumpled and collapsed in on itself. There was one dormer window that watched me like a hooded eye.

I'd seen enough.

I was turning Skyrocket around to go home when his hooves sank into the ground. I remembered Abel's words about getting swamped in. It didn't look like a bog, which I thought would be like a big pit of mud. This swamp was just kind of lumpy with oozy-looking places around clumps of grass.

"Come on, boy," I urged, yanking at Skyrocket's bridle. He floundered and the saddle began to slip. I had visions of it turning down under his belly and me being tromped to death. Mom and Dad would be sorry they had ever brought me to Blue Creek when they found my poor, bruised body.

If they ever found me. Nobody knew I was up there.

Each of Skyrocket's leaps drove him deeper into the mushy ground. I thought of vaulting off his back. But would I just sink into the swamp too?

"Help!" I screeched.

"Let him have his head," a voice said. "Stop pulling on the bridle."

I snapped my head around and saw the guy who had been under the trees the day we arrived. He still wore the same clothes and still looked as if he might run away at any moment. He stood over where the ground was firm and continued to give me instructions.

"Hang onto the saddle horn," he said. "Let the horse get out of there himself."

I did what he said, grateful for any advice. In a series

of leaps, Skyrocket pulled himself out of the bog and gained his footing near the guy.

"Thanks," I said, as both Skyrocket and I panted away our fright. "I'm lucky you were here."

"I'm always here," he said. "I'm Gideon. The resident ghost."

Chapter Three

I stepped backward. Maybe it was because of the way that old house scowled at me. Or maybe it was the absolute seriousness of Gideon's face as he said he was a ghost.

For just a moment I believed him.

The whole scene was unreal. It spooked me, and that's what made me step backward. I realized it was a mistake when I felt my foot sink into the slime of the swamp.

"Watch out," Gideon said. "You're getting into trouble again."

He made no move to help me.

I windmilled my arms to keep my balance. I still held Skyrocket's bridle reins, and my frantic movements startled him. He yanked back, eyes rolling. That's what saved me. As Skyrocket took up the slack, he pulled me onto firm ground again.

Gideon watched. "That was a close call. You should watch where you're putting your feet."

That ticked me. "You scared me with that ghost stuff. Do you get your jollies that way? Do you make your living saving people from the swamp?"

A flicker crossed his face. It could have been a smile.

"Make my living?" he repeated. "That's an odd thing to say to a ghost."

I kicked my foot to get the slime off. "Well, *pardon* me. I don't know the proper etiquette. I've never met a ghost before."

"Not many people have."

"I could have done without the honor." I glared at him.

Gideon gazed steadily back. "You wouldn't have seen me at all if you hadn't been in trouble."

"So why didn't you lend me a hand and help to pull me out instead of just standing there bellowing orders?" The guy was really getting to me.

"I'm a ghost," he said. "What good could I have done?"

I stared at him. He looked substantial enough. Broad shoulders under that strange jacket he wore. High, laced boots. Tall—close to six feet, I guessed. What did he mean, what good could he have done?

As if he read my mind, he stretched out a hand. "Have you ever touched a ghost? Or tried to?"

I moved to take his hand, then stopped. The old house behind him watched. Trees bent close to it, whispering into its empty windows. There was a mustiness in the air, and I could hear Skyrocket's nervous breathing.

What if this was real? What if I took his hand—and it wasn't there? What if I touched only empty air?

I choked down the sudden panic that rose in my throat. "You're serious about this, aren't you."

"*Dead* serious." For the first time he actually did smile, showing large, even teeth. A cloud passed in front of the sun, making his deep-set eyes look hollow.

Like a skull.

"I have to go." I moved to Skyrocket's solid warmth,

putting a foot in the stirrup. The leather creaked as I pulled my weight up.

"Don't go," Gideon said. "I won't hurt you. I'd like to talk."

What could I say to a ghost? How are things in the old cemetery these days? Met any new protoplasm lately?

"Tell me who you really are and maybe I'll stay." I looked down at him from my perch on the horse.

"I can't tell you any more. Even ghosts have secrets, you know."

His hair was thick and dark brown. He couldn't be a ghost. Probably a first-class nut case. I ought to get out of there, I thought. Nobody knew I was up there at the old house. He could murder me and throw me into the swamp and no one would ever know.

"My mother will be wondering where I am." I patted the bulging saddle bag. "She needs these things in a hurry. I just came from the store."

"Sure," he said. "How could she get through the afternoon without an emergency nip of vinegar?"

His grin widened.

How did he know what I had in that saddle bag?

Panic flooded me. I dug my heels into Skyrocket's sides. It didn't take a lot of urging to get him started this time. He sprang to life, as eager as I was to get out of there. His hooves clattered on the rocks as we circled around the swamp and headed down the narrow valley alongside the creek.

"Come back sometime, Ashley." Gideon's voice was like an echo.

I didn't look back until Skyrocket and I got up to the jutting hillside that would hide us from Gideon's view. Then I turned.

He was gone.

Had he ever really been there?

It wasn't until then that another little terror hit me, like a mini-electric shock.

How did he know my name?

Once we got to the rutted old road, Skyrocket broke into a jolting trot. I didn't care, so long as he got me home in a hurry. I was going to tell Mom and Dad that there was no way I would stay in a place that was haunted.

Maybe Gideon could be my ticket back to California — and Richard.

Skyrocket was sweaty by the time we got to the barn. Abel was there, and I wondered if I should try my hysteria out on him. As I slid from the horse, I visualized bursting into the house, sobbing wildly, supported by Abel.

But I scrubbed that idea when I saw him eyeing Skyrocket's muddy legs. He'd warned me about going up there where the creeks meet. Why hadn't he mentioned a ghost?

I thought things over. Both of my parents were scientific-minded. I'd probably have a better chance of convincing them to let me leave if I built up a few facts and presented my case logically. Calmly.

I took a couple of deep breaths to slow down my heart.

"I went up there." I waved my arm in the direction of the old house. "Skyrocket bogged down."

"Noticed that," Abel said. "Know how to cool down a horse when he's warm?"

The abrupt switch of subjects threw me off track. "Uh . . . I guess so. Walk him around, then wipe him off." I'd learned that much at Roving Rangers Day Camp.

Abel leaned against the barn as I led Skyrocket around in circles. I felt that I'd lost all my momentum. Maybe if

I'd tried the hysteria, I might have learned something from Abel.

After a few rounds, he brought some clean rags from the barn. Handing one to me, he bent to work on Skyrocket's muddy legs.

I began wiping the horse's neck and back.

"Racine Wisconsin told me there was a haunted house up there where the creeks meet," I began. "I mean LeeAnne McFadden. That's her real name. She calls herself Racine now."

Abel nodded. "Spring Breeze before that. Once she was Otilie LeClare. Don't seem to know *who* she is."

"Abel," I broke in. "About the house—is it true it's haunted?"

"See any ghosts?"

"I saw a guy who said he was a ghost. Told me how to get Skyrocket out of the swamp."

"Helpful," Abel stated.

"Have you seen him? Is he for real?"

"Look real?"

"Looked like an ordinary guy in funny clothes." I was beginning to talk like Abel.

"How's a ghost supposed to look?"

I shrugged. "He said his name was Gideon."

Abel nodded, still bent over, wiping mud from Skyrocket's leg.

"Gideon Glessing," he said.

Glessing? Hadn't Abel said that name the day we arrived?

"Is he related to George Glessing, the guy the hill was named after?"

"Brother."

It wasn't easy digging information from Abel.

"So who named the hill George?"

"Gid did."

I looked at Abel under Skyrocket's belly. "Gideon named the hill after his brother? Why?"

"Memorial, maybe. He thought he caused George's death." Abel didn't even pause in his methodical cleaning.

I was beginning to feel cold prickles at the back of my neck again.

"When did that happen?"

Abel paused, gazing toward George Hill. "Nineteen-oh-nine. That's the year on George's gravestone."

I thought of Gideon's clothes. Were they what a young guy would have worn in 1909?

"How did it happen?"

Abel settled back on his heels. "Heard tell that they went swimming together in Bear River. Just across George Hill there. Gideon was always a rowdy one. Show-off. Dared George to swim across the river. George wasn't much of a swimmer, but he always tried to keep up with his older brother."

Abel moved to Skyrocket's back legs and began cleaning again.

"So what happened?"

"Gid made it. George didn't."

I thought about that. "So I'd think George would haunt the old house. Not Gideon."

Abel shook his head. "Gideon was all broke up about it. Whole family was. They moved away. Gid used to come back and camp out there, calling for George in the night. Got married eventually. Brought his wife and kids back here to live. Finally died. Just sorrowed away. That's what his wife said."

"How old was he when he died?"

"Young."

"How young?" If he said seventeen, I was going to get chills. That's about how old the guy at the house looked.

But he'd just said Gideon had been married. So he couldn't have been that young.

"About thirty-eight when he died. Maybe forty," Abel said.

I breathed easier.

"He was about seventeen when George died."

I got the chills.

I didn't tell Mom and Dad about Gideon that night. I don't really know why. Maybe because I felt sympathy for that pathetic ghost—if that's what he was—sorrowing away over the death of his brother. If I started blabbing about a ghost on our property, Mom and Dad would investigate. They'd go to the house and find out what was going on. Do tests. Psych Gideon out. Disturb the dead.

No, it would be better if I found out a little more about him myself first. That way, he could be of more use to me.

Chapter Four

The next day I got a letter from Val. I stood out by the mailbox at the end of the driveway to read it.

It wasn't good news.

"Ashley, come home," it said in huge letters at the top of the page. Val's dad has a Macintosh computer that can do anything. Under the first line, in smaller letters, it said, "Richard is in DANGER!"

My eyes hurried down the page, dreading to read what the danger was.

"Maybe I shouldn't even worry you this way," Val went on. "But I thought you'd want to KNOW. Mike told me that Eddie told him that Cindy told him that Lisa told her that Jennifer told her that MONIQUE McBRIDE told her she's putting the move on Richard."

Monique McBride! I groaned. When Val said "DANGER!" I'd thought physical, like having Hulk Hazelton mad at him or something. But Monique was WORSE! Monique played the part of Stupefyin' Jones in our high school's production of *Li'l Abner,* and she didn't even have to act.

I could visualize her riding in MY place in that red truck

of Richard's, her long black hair fanning out in the breeze. She probably even liked guns.

I looked in the mailbox again, hoping a letter from Richard had appeared there since I'd last looked. I'd sent two letters to him since we left California. There'd been time for him to answer.

But the only things still in the mailbox were an electric bill forwarded from home and a piece of junk mail saying we might be the lucky winners of six million dollars.

Richard was a man of action, not a letter writer. I knew that.

Maybe he'd call me, instead.

Maybe I should call him.

Sighing, I read the rest of Val's letter as I walked to the house. She'd had her hair cut. Lisa told her that Cindy told her that Eddie told her he really liked it that way. Eddie was the guy she was interested in.

She said she really missed me and wished I could be there for the big beach bash they were throwing on Saturday. She ended with, "Come BACK. You can live with ME."

I felt very sorry for myself. Monique was after MY guy, and everybody I knew was living it up with beach parties while the only person I had to talk to was a ghost in a swamp.

Well, if I had to, I would use that ghost somehow to get myself back to civilization. So what if Mom and Dad dissected him? He was a *ghost*. He had no life to live, the way I did.

"Mom," I said as I charged into the house, "Mom, there's something I want to talk with you about."

Mom was making bread, mixing it with her hands. She was elbow deep in flour and looked happy.

"Oh, Ashley," she said, "I wondered where you were. You got a call from Racine, Wisconsin. Who'd be calling you from there?"

I couldn't help smiling. "Racine Wisconsin is a girl, Mom. I met her at the general store yesterday."

Mom paused in her bread mixing to stare at me. "Who'd name a girl Racine Wisconsin?"

"She named herself. Her real name's LeeAnne McFadden, but she says that doesn't make a statement." I wondered what I could learn from Racine about Gideon.

Mom looked puzzled, but then she shrugged and said, "Anyway, you're supposed to call back. Any interesting mail?"

I handed her the bill and the six-million-dollar envelope. "I got a letter from Val."

Mom eyed the letter I held up. "So what did she have to say?"

I considered my options. I could let Mom read Val's letter. But then she'd know why I wanted to hurry back to California and that would scrub the whole idea for sure. Or I could tell her about the beach party that was coming up and how much I needed to be there with my friends.

I could blurt out the whole thing about Gideon and say I wasn't about to live in the near vicinity of a ghost and that Val had invited me to stay with her family.

It was like one of those multiple choice questions on an exam—the answer would be a, b, c, all of the above, or none of the above.

I opted for none of the above. I would talk to Racine before I told my folks about Gideon. But I'd be careful about what I told her. I was new here. She might think I was weird if I announced I'd seen a ghost already.

"Val said she cut her hair," I told Mom.

I called Racine Wisconsin.

"Can you come over?" she said. "I'm stuck here with the kids for the day, but I'd sure like to say something besides 'wipe your nose' and 'don't eat the dog food.' "

I laughed. "Sure, I can come, Racine. Right now?"

"The sooner the better. Do you have wheels?"

"I have hooves. I'll saddle up Skyrocket and we may hit your place by about Christmas."

"I'll send Whit to get you if you'd like," she said.

The thought of riding anywhere with her sullen husband was less appealing than jouncing along on Skyrocket.

"Thanks," I said, "but Skyrocket and I will make it. You said to turn right at the old schoolhouse, right?"

"Right is right," she said. "Look for a two-story, salmon-colored brick house with a balcony."

It wasn't too hard to find Racine's house. It stood surrounded by a broad tree-shaded lawn as if it had been there a long time.

Racine was on the front lawn, watching for me. Petey John and Fuffer were both there playing on the grass, and three other stair-step little kids as well. Two large dogs frisked around in the midst of the kids.

"Hi," Racine called as Skyrocket clopped into the yard. "Tie him up there by the watering trough and come join us. We've got Kool-Aid and chocolate chip cookies waiting."

I saw the card table set up under a tree. It was covered with a rough orange cloth and held a tall, galvanized water cooler, a brown earthenware bowl, paper cups, and a neat stack of yellow napkins. It looked very inviting.

Petey John was hanging on the edge of the table. "You better hurry," he said. He was obviously about to have a snack attack.

I slid from Skyrocket's back and tied him to the moss-covered water trough. He immediately stuck his nose into it and began sucking up water with loud, slurpy noises.

As I walked across the lawn, Racine ran to the porch and clattered a metal rod around a black iron triangle.

"Refreshments," she bellowed.

That brought more kids. They appeared from behind the house, around the barn, and across the road. They stared curiously at me.

I stared back, counting silently.

Racine laughed as she hurried to fill paper cups. "Kind of takes your breath away, doesn't it?"

"Yes. If you don't mind my asking, how many of them are yours?"

"Most of them." She handed me the first overflowing paper cup. "All of the redheads and a couple of the blonds. The rest are neighborhood kids. They congregate here."

I took a sip of the Kool-Aid. It slid down my throat, cool and sweet and cherry-flavored. Over the rim of the cup, I stared at the kids. Some of the red-haired ones seemed not much younger than Racine.

When the kids all wore little red, upturned smiles from the Kool-Aid, Racine filled a cup for herself and put a handful of cookies in a napkin. "Come on over to the porch," she said. "We'll talk while we keep an eye on the troops."

We sat down in white wicker rocking chairs. "You seem awfully young to have so many kids," I said.

Racine choked on her drink. "Good grief," she sputtered, "you didn't think they were *mine*, did you?"

I nodded sheepishly. "I guess I got the wrong impression at the store yesterday. You know—the way you were handling Petey John and Fuffer."

Racine laughed, a gurgly, fun kind of laugh. "The kids are my brothers and sisters, Ashley. My folks have nine kids. They're in town today checking with the doctor about the arrival of number ten. She should be here in a few days."

"She? How do you know it will be a girl?" I bit into one of the chocolate chip cookies Racine offered. It was chewy and still slightly warm from the oven.

"It's the pattern," Racine said. "See, in our family we have Whit, me, Thayne, Delmer, Raydawn, LaVere, Malora, Petey John, and Fuffer. His real name is Christopher, but Fuffer is what Petey John called him for a long time. Anyway, that's boy, girl, boy, boy, girl, then the same pattern again: boy, girl, boy, boy. That means this one has to be a girl. Don't you think things run in patterns?"

"I never thought about it," I said.

Just then Racine waved toward the barn. "Hey, Whitwood," she yelled. "Come and join us in some junk food."

I turned to see the guy named Whit coming from the barn. Obviously, he was Racine's brother. I could see that now. They both had the same dark auburn hair and blue eyes.

I was glad I hadn't said something dumb about thinking he was her husband.

Today Whit wore blue jeans and a white T-shirt. He had strong-looking arms, like Richard. But I guessed that Whit's muscles came from the hard work he did on the farm rather than lifting weights, the way Richard's did.

He got himself some cookies and punch, then came over to lean on the porch railing while he ate.

"You remember each other, I guess," Racine said.

"Sure." Whit nodded. "How's it going?" He sounded bored.

"Fine." I tried to match his tone.

I wondered why he didn't like me.

Whit didn't stay long. He refilled his punch cup twice, scarfed a dozen cookies, then went back to the barn.

"Your horse is loose," he called as he passed the watering trough where Skyrocket stood. "You better learn how to tie a knot." He retied the horse's reins. He seemed to disapprove of everything about me.

"Don't mind him," Racine said. "He's kind of cranky around girls. Especially city girls."

Of course I had to ask why.

"A girl from Phoenix took him for a ride last summer," Racine said. She paused long enough to yell a warning to one of the little kids, who was swinging upside down from a tree limb. "She was staying with some relatives here in town. She was really Whit's first girlfriend, and he thought they had this big romance going. But she dumped him like a dirty sock when a guy from her hometown came through with his fancy car." Racine munched a cookie. "Let's not talk about him. I want to hear about you. How do you like it here so far?"

"It's different from California," I said.

"Good or bad?"

I thought "All bad," but what I said was, "There's not a whole lot going on here."

"You just haven't got involved yet," Racine said. "There's an innertubing party at the river on Saturday. Whit and I will take you with us to that. Then there's a rodeo on the Fourth of July, and we have a picnic and dance on Pioneer Day."

I'd go with them to the innertubing party, just for something to do. But if I was lucky, I wouldn't be there for any of the other events.

"I rode up to the old house yesterday after I talked with you," I said.

"So you've already initiated yourself," Racine said. "We usually initiate all newcomers by taking them up there at midnight to meet Gideon the ghost. Did you see him by any chance?"

I was surprised. Maybe my experience hadn't been unusual. "Do new people usually see him?"

Racine laughed, that happy, gurgly laugh again. "Some think they do, by the time we finish telling them all our ghost stories. But he hasn't really appeared to anybody for a long, long time."

I remembered how Gideon had said I wouldn't have seen him if I hadn't been in danger.

"So you didn't answer my question," Racine said. "Did you see him?"

"What's he supposed to look like?" I countered.

Racine shrugged. "I've never seen him. But my great-grandfather said he looked just like he did the day his brother drowned. Do you know the story?"

I nodded. "Abel Morehead told me."

"Well, he's supposed to wear some old black pants and a short jacket and one of those caps like cab drivers wear in movies."

I felt pale.

Racine got to her feet. "I can show you how he's supposed to look. Come on inside with me."

I followed her into the house. We went through a large, sunny kitchen that looked as if it was from another century, except for the electrical appliances. There were braided rugs on the floor and starched white curtains at the windows. A huge round oak table occupied the center of the room.

Racine led me into the dark, cool living room where oval-shaped photographs of what I assumed were her ancestors stared down at us from the walls. The Mc-Faddens must have liked having their pictures taken, because there were at least a dozen of them.

Racine went to a doily-covered, claw-footed table and opened a photograph album. It was one of the old-fashioned kind that have thick pages with the photo inserted in the center.

She flipped through the album, then stopped. "Here," she said. "This is a picture of my great-grandfather with Gideon and George Glessing. It was taken about a week before George drowned."

I hesitated to look. But I had no idea how to explain why I didn't want to.

My eyes followed Racine's pointing finger. The photo showed three young guys standing by a tree. One was tall and skinny, with a grin like Whit's. Another looked younger, with dark hair and deep-set eyes.

The third guy wore wide-legged black pants, a short jacket, and a cap with a bill.

I shifted my eyes to his face.

It *was* Gideon—the same Gideon I had seen at the old house.

Chapter Five

I guess I gasped or something, because Racine asked, "Is something wrong, Ashley?"

Was it time to admit I'd seen Gideon? No. No, I needed to know more.

I jabbed a finger at the picture of her great-grandfather and said, "I think it's amazing how much he looks like Whit."

"That's Racine's Law. Things tend to recur." She grinned, then looked closely at me. "Are you sure that's all that's bugging you? Did something happen at the old house yesterday? Ashley, have you seen Gideon?"

I returned her grin. "What makes you think Gideon would suddenly appear to me when no one else has seen him for so many years?"

She must have known I was beating around the bush, but all she said was, "Wow, it would really be neat if he's around again. Everybody knows about Blue Creek's haunted house. We could set up a hotdog stand for all the tourists."

Laughing, she shut the old album and situated it neatly in the middle of the claw-footed table.

I wondered how Gideon would react to a tourist invasion of the old house.

"Let's go back to the porch," Racine said. "I don't dare leave the kids alone for very long."

As we eased ourselves down into the white rockers again, she yelled, "Raydawn! Watch Fuffer. He's into the dog food again." She grinned at me. "One of these days that kid's going to start barking."

It was shady there on the porch, and the light came through the heavy vines with a greenish tinge. Just like the way it was under the drooping trees by the old house.

"Racine," I said, "exactly how long has it been since anyone has seen the famous ghost?"

She leaned back in the rocker, making it creak like old bones. "Well, let's see. I don't think anybody's seen him for sure since my great-grandfather's time. A lot of people have said they thought they *might* have seen him." Again she gave me that close look. "So I guess it's been over fifty years."

Maybe it was the greenish light, or maybe the quietness of the summer day with the voices of the kids coming across the broad lawn like echoes, but something was giving me an eerie feeling.

"Was there any special reason why he appeared then?" I asked. "Fifty years ago, I mean?"

Racine kept an eye on the tangle of kids. "You know all the background details?"

"Abel told me how George drowned," I said. "And how Gideon felt it was his fault and all."

Racine nodded. Her voice fell to that soft monotone people use when they're telling ghost stories.

"My great-grandfather said that the only time he ever saw Gideon was one day when he was cutting firewood up there by the old house. He chopped down a quaking aspen tree, and it fell the wrong way. He would have been hurt—except he thought he heard somebody whispering to him to get out of the way. Then he said there was a dim shape over by the house. He figured it was Gideon. He got a good conk on the head, but that was all. It's written down in an old diary that's around here someplace."

I put two and two together. "So he's supposed to appear to people who are in danger."

Racine nodded again. "Since he couldn't save his brother, they say he tries to help other people. Were you in danger up there at the old house, Ashley?"

I wasn't expecting the question and I blurted out, "Yes." I started to say that I didn't want to go up to the old house again, but just then Racine stood up and waved.

"There are my parents," she said. "Now I can turn the troops over to them and we can go."

I stood up too and watched the battered blue van turn into the yard and stop in a cloud of dust. A tall, blond man got out of the driver's seat and hurried around to open the door for a red-haired woman wearing a fresh-looking blue and white maternity dress.

For some reason I'd expected Racine's mother to be large and shapeless and tired, with maybe flat feet and an aching back. But she was small and slender, except for the coming baby, and she sprang from the van as if she had energy to spare. She waved to the kids, who flowed to meet her in a stream of blue jeans. Even Racine ran across the lawn to greet her parents. Whit came from the barn, and everyone talked at once, setting up a chatter as cheerful as the clucking of the hens in the coop nearby.

Several of the kids began towing Mrs. McFadden to-

ward the house, pointing at me. Others stayed to help
Whit and Mr. McFadden pull bulging bags of groceries
from the van.

"Mom," Racine said as the clump of people came up
to me, "this is Ashley. Ashley, this is my mom."

From my place on the porch, I looked down into a pair
of eyes as blue as Racine's. (The operation of Racine's Law
again!)

"Ashley! How nice to meet you." Mrs. McFadden
smiled, sounding as if she really was pleased. "You're from
that new family in town." Up close, I saw she had a broad
scar on her cheek.

I nodded. "We live on the old Eskelsen place."

Mrs. McFadden's grin was a lot like Racine's. "I wasn't
going to say that. You must get tired of hearing your home
referred to as somebody else's place."

I thought of saying that it didn't matter much to me
because it wasn't really my home. But instead, I just smiled.
I liked Mrs. McFadden. Usually when I meet the parents
of one of my friends, I relegate them to faceless nonentity.
Parents. But Mrs. McFadden was a real person. Maybe
because she saw me as a real person, not just a generic
teenager.

"Come on in, Ashley," she said, "and we'll talk after
we unload all the groceries."

I didn't see how she was going to talk with all the kids
pulling at her dress. I followed everyone inside just as a
small army began to arrive with enough groceries to stock
a store.

Mrs. McFadden was like a general, directing the army
about where to put what. "Raydawn, put all the milk in
the fridge. Thayne and Delmer, carry those bags of canned
goods down to the cellar and put everything on shelves.

LaVere, wash those grapes and put them in a big bowl to take outside under the trees."

So that's how she dispatched the kids. When all the bags were empty, they went outside to eat the grapes.

Whit stayed only long enough to gulp down a handful of grapes, scowl at me, and say he'd be out in the barn if anybody needed him.

I was introduced to Mr. McFadden, who smiled amiably, but I could see that to him I was just another of the many kids who hung around his home. He left soon to join Whit.

After everyone was gone, Racine said, "Mom, you'd better put your feet up."

"Right." Mrs. McFadden headed toward the cool living room. "But you girls come along too, so Ashley can tell me about the world outside our hills."

We sat on the old-fashioned sofas under the watchful eyes of the ancestors on the wall. Mrs. McFadden shifted around a little to get comfortable. "I'll be glad when the baby's here," she said.

Looking at her and the pictures, I had an odd feeling of the past, present, and future all coming together right there.

"I like the old pictures on your walls," I said. "My mom would freak out over them. She's a genealogy nut, but we don't have any pictures older than her grandparents."

Mrs. McFadden leaned back to look over her head. "Some of them are my ancestors and some are my husband's. Isn't it interesting to think that if it weren't for them, we wouldn't be here today?" She pointed at a picture of a man with a long beard. Next to him was the photograph of a youngish-looking woman with her hair pulled back in a bun. "They're the ones who built this house. Four generations of McFaddens have lived in it so far." She shifted around again, then said, "Well, Ashley, let's hear about you."

"Mom," Racine interrupted, "Ashley and I are going up to the old haunted house before it gets dark. Ashley saw something up there yesterday."

I wished she hadn't said that, but I didn't think it would do any good to deny it now. Besides, Mrs. McFadden had a very interesting reaction to it. She didn't change position, but I had the impression that her whole body suddenly came to full alert.

Her voice didn't give anything away, though, as she said, "Oh? What did you see, Ashley?"

I wanted to talk to her about Gideon. But I was afraid Racine would be steamed at me for not telling her everything. And besides, if she found out that I really *had* seen Gideon, she'd probably tell all her friends and the tourist invasion would begin.

"I saw what would make a great movie set for a haunted house," I told Mrs. McFadden.

She gazed at me, her blue eyes seeming to peel away layers down to the inner me. I knew she knew I knew more than I was telling.

"Isn't there some other place Ashley would rather see?" Mrs. McFadden asked Racine.

Racine shook her head. "If the ghost's around, I want to see him before he goes into hibernation for another fifty years. So we're going up there."

I hoped Mrs. McFadden would say we shouldn't go there, that we shouldn't disturb the poor ghost, that we should stay away from haunted houses.

But all she said was, "Be careful of the bog."

Racine saddled a horse named Floss and we were on our way back down the road past the yellow schoolhouse and up the narrow valley where I lived. Racine chattered on about what there was to do in Blue Creek and how things picked up once school started and all the kids were bused to Prentiss.

"You'll be going to Prentiss High in the fall, won't you, Ashley?" she asked.

"No." I shook my head firmly. "No, I'll be back in California long before that." I didn't mention that I might even be married.

"Really?" Racine sounded impressed. "Will your folks let you go back by yourself?"

"It's *my* life," I said stiffly. "I can do with it what I want."

Racine bounced a little on her horse. "Maybe I'll go, too. Then we could get an apartment together, just the two of us."

"Would your folks let you do that?"

She laughed. "Are you kidding? But it's fun to think about. Sometimes I get the feeling that I'm just a link in the long chain of McFaddens, without any identity of my own. I'm there to watch the kids and do the laundry and dust all those pictures. Sometimes I wonder if they ever really see me." She tossed her hair back. "I'd really like to break away and do something crazy. That's why I change my name so often, so I'll remember I'm me, with at least that much control over my own life."

I could understand the way she felt.

We were clopping past the long driveway that led to my house. I wondered if Racine could be detoured from continuing on this trip.

"Why don't you come in and meet my family?" I said.

"There's cold milk in the fridge, and Mom is always making cookies for my brothers."

Racine pulled the reins of her horse to stop. "How old are your brothers?"

"Nine and six. You wouldn't be interested, unless you like to build dams in the creek and play Monopoly."

Racine reactivated Floss by slapping the reins against her neck. "I guess I'd rather meet Gideon."

In a few minutes we were under the big trees that reached green fingers down to trail across our shoulders. It was even gloomier than the day before because the light was beginning to fade. The sun set early in the narrow little valley with its ring of high mountains.

"Ashley," Racine said, "I just remembered you said you were in danger here yesterday. What kind of danger?"

"The swamp." I pointed ahead of us. "I rode Skyrocket right into it."

Racine guided Floss straight for the swamp.

"Racine!" I yelled. "Watch where you're going."

Racine kept going. When Floss felt her feet sinking into the soft ground, she stopped, tossing her head. But Racine urged her on until her hooves sank deep and she heaved her big body from side to side to get out of the muck.

"Help!" Racine yelled.

I looked toward the old house. There was no sign of Gideon.

Floss lurched ahead, trying find solid footing. Racine was having a hard time staying aboard.

"It's deeper than I thought," she said. "Floss can't get out."

"Gideon!" I called.

The old house watched silently.

It was up to me.

Sliding from Skyrocket's back, I ran to the edge of the swamp. Skyrocket took the opportunity to head for home, his hooves making little puffs of dust as he trotted. It was the most energy he'd displayed since I'd met him.

"Racine," I said as calmly as I could, "let go of the reins and hang onto the saddle horn. Let Floss figure out how to do it."

But Floss must not have been as smart as Skyrocket, because she didn't head for the firm territory.

I took a couple of steps out onto the boggy ground. I sank in, but not as deep as the horse because I was lighter. A couple more steps took me close enough to get hold of Floss's bridle.

"Come on, Floss," I coaxed. "You can do it."

With a lurch and a heave, Floss pulled her feet out of the slime and got to solid ground. Racine jumped from her back.

"Now I know what it means to be bogged down," she said.

Her flippancy ticked me off. "You could have hurt yourself," I scolded, "and the horse, too. Why did you go into the swamp deliberately?"

Racine looked sheepish. "Well, somebody has to be in danger for Gideon to appear. It was dumb of me, but I didn't think the swamp was quite that dangerous." She patted Floss's neck. "Did Gideon wade out to help you yesterday?"

"No," I said. "He stayed there under the tree and told me what to do."

"Aha!" Racine's eyes glinted. "So you do admit seeing him."

She'd trapped me. "Yes. But I won't tell anybody about your being so foolish as to ride right into the swamp if you won't tell anybody about my being weird enough to see ghosts."

She grinned at me. "Deal. Now let's get out of here. I've lost interest in seeing Gideon."

I was restless that night. I wished I'd hear from Richard. Had Monique McBride gotten to him? Was it a case of "out of sight, out of mind"? Should I call him, tell him I'd marry him? Life would be meaningless without Richard.

Finn and Truman, tired from their day of dam building and mud puddling, went to bed early. Mom and Dad were watching a documentary on TV.

I went outside. The moon was riding on top of George Hill, providing plenty of light for me to see my way. I needed to walk. But the shadows were long and there were owls hooting somewhere in the darkness near the barn. I was a little spooked and didn't want to go too far.

I decided to walk down along the driveway to the mailbox and back. At least that was familiar territory.

I was on the old stone bridge listening to the soft whisper of water underneath when Gideon appeared by my side. I hadn't heard any footsteps. He was just there.

"Hello, Ashley," he said.

Chapter Six

I felt like a startled cat, with every sense suddenly alert. My fingers curled as if I had claws. If I'd had a tail, it would have puffed to three times its size. Adrenaline whipped me around and put my feet into gear.

"Don't go," Gideon said. "I just want to talk."

I ran about ten steps before turning. My heart pumped blood into my arms and legs, making them tingle.

"Gideon!" I gasped. "You scared me out of my wits!"

I could see his white teeth in the moonlight as he gave me that wide, skull-like grin. "I guess that's one of the hazards of being a ghost." He walked toward me. "I'm sorry, Ashley."

I panted a little to drain off the excess energy the adrenaline had provided. "Well, don't just materialize from nowhere like that."

I looked at his feet to see if maybe he was floating, which would explain how he could move so silently. But no, those odd, high-laced boots of his were making definite prints in the soft dust.

Prints? Do ghosts make footprints?

"What did you want to talk about?" I asked.

"About 'shoes—and ships—and sealing wax—Of cab-bages—and kings,' " Gideon said.

I recognized that as a line from "The Walrus and the Carpenter." We'd studied Lewis Carroll in ninth grade.

"Well, well," I said, "aren't we literary? I didn't know ghosts were allowed to read."

He shrugged. "We have to do something. It gets a little tiresome dragging chains across attics and whoo-whooing in the dark all the time."

He was teasing me.

"What was it you wanted to talk about, really?" I asked.

"Let's sit down and I'll tell you." He walked back to the bridge and hoisted himself up onto the stone wall, patting the space next to him.

Part of me wanted to run to the house, my tongue clanging like an alarm bell. If my parents came out and actually saw Gideon themselves, maybe they'd know we couldn't stay in this ghost-infested place.

But the other part of me was curious.

Curiosity won.

I walked back to the bridge and tried to climb up onto the wall.

"How about giving me a hand?" I said.

He laughed. "You might as well grab a handful of air. I'm a ghost. Remember?"

"Oh, come off it, Gideon," I said. "You're as solid as I am. You were making footprints in the dust."

He put out his hand, the way he'd done at the old house when I was in the swamp. "Want to test me?"

Behind and below me I could hear the creek chuckle as it flowed under the bridge. Somewhere in the dark trees near the barn a mourning dove, or maybe an owl, gave a hollow cry.

Footprints or no footprints, I didn't want my hand passing through empty space when my eyes told me there was a body there. Maybe the next time I saw him in the daylight I'd try it. Not now.

I scraped my knee, scrambling up onto the stone wall. I rubbed it as I settled down and turned to Gideon. "Okay, talk."

"I wanted to thank you," he said, "for not broadcasting it around that I'm here."

"You took a chance, letting me see you," I said. "I could very well have told everybody."

He nodded. "You could have. But I figured you wouldn't, being new in town and all. You wouldn't want the other kids thinking you're weird." He smiled at me.

"What would have happened if I *had* told?"

"I would have left," he said. "I don't want to see anybody. Except you."

I didn't know whether to feel honored or scared. "Racine knows you're here. She guessed from some of the things I said."

He nodded again. "I saw her. You did a good job of getting her out of the swamp."

"You know Racine?"

"I've seen her a few times. She hasn't seen me."

"But you watched our struggles in the swamp. Why didn't you come to her rescue, the way you came to mine? Aren't you supposed to appear when someone is in danger?"

"Is that what Racine told you?"

"She said that's what people believe. She said the last time you appeared was when her great-grandfather was about to be clobbered by a tree and he heard you telling him to get out of the way. He thought he saw you too."

Gideon looked down at his feet. "He probably saw a shadow and heard the wind in the branches of the tree as it started to fall."

"So it's not true, what they say."

"People make up things," Gideon said.

"Then why did you appear to me?"

"You're in danger. I don't want you to be hurt."

"So it *is* true."

I could see that skull-like grin again in the dim light.

I thought back to what he'd said. "You mean I *was* in danger. There in the swamp."

"I mean you *are* in danger, Ashley."

I thought I'd used up my whole supply of adrenaline, but it was pouring into my bloodstream again.

"What do you mean?" I asked hoarsely.

"You could trash your whole future," he said. "I want to help you."

"What do you know about my future?" My teeth were chattering now. "What do you know about anything? What makes you think you can help me, or that I even want help? It's *my* life. It's *my* business what I do with it."

He shook his head. "It's not your life alone, Ashley. Don't you see? What you do affects others, just as much as it does you. It affects the future, right on down through the generations."

I thought of the dark, gloomy pictures of Racine's ancestors hanging on the wall of their house. I thought of her great-grandfather who had known Gideon.

Nothing made sense. How did Gideon know what plans I had? What was I doing standing there in the darkness talking to a ghost?

This time I did run, my feet stirring up small duststorms as they whapped the ground.

I burst into the house and stood panting in the hall.

Mom looked up from the TV. "Ashley, what's the matter? You look as if you've seen a ghost."

They'd never believe me. Not yet. Not enough to move back to California.

"I've just been running in the moonlight," I said, and went upstairs to bed.

On Saturday the mail came before Racine and Whit arrived to get me for the innertubing party on the river, and joy, joy, joy, there was a letter from Richard. It was short. I knew how Richard hated to write letters. But it said enough.

"I miss you so very much, Ashley," it said. "It's only been a little over a week that you've been gone, but it seems like an eternity. I've been trying to decide what to do about it."

"Oh, Richard," I groaned. "What *can* we do?"

I wondered how much longer it would take for me to build up enough evidence about Gideon, the ghost, to convince Mom and Dad to move back to California. I had a worse thought: would the evidence convince them, or would Mom just get involved in trying to do something for that poor, forlorn ghost, if that's what he was?

Suddenly I had a new thought. Why hadn't I thought of it before? If I couldn't go home to Richard, why couldn't Richard come to Blue Creek?

Humming happily, I hugged his letter against my chest and walked to the house. I would call him, maybe after the tubing party. Or perhaps on Sunday. I would tell him to come.

I was ready when Racine and Whit came to pick me up for the party. Racine got out of the van to let me in.

"We'll put you in the middle," she said. "Maybe you'll warm up Whit's hormones."

Whit scowled, and I tried not to touch him as I slid across the torn plastic seat to the center. I didn't care if Racine twitted me about him. I had no interest in him one way or another. It was obvious that the feeling was mutual.

Before we could leave, Finn and Truman spotted us. They'd been working on their dam-building project since early morning. They were barefoot and dirty and happy.

"Can we go?" Finn asked politely.

"You don't even know where we're going," I said.

"We'd go anywhere." Finn's nose was running and he scrubbed across it with his arm. It didn't help his appearance much.

"Sorry, guys." Whit's scowl faded and he spoke gently. "This trip isn't for kids. You don't see any of my brothers and sisters here, do you?"

"Who's she?" Truman pointed at Racine.

"She's my sister," Whit said. "But I mean kids your age."

Finn and Truman looked interested.

"You got kids our age?" Truman asked.

Whit nodded. "More than you can count."

"Tell your mother to take you over to our house," Racine said. "The kids were getting together for Run Sheep Run when we left."

Truman smiled. "I like sheep."

"It's a game," said the World's Greatest Authority.

Truman looked disappointed.

Whit started the car. "We have to go. Take it easy, guys."

Finn and Truman waved as we drove over the stone bridge and out to the highway.

"They're neat kids," Whit said.

It was the first cordial thing he'd said to me.

"I guess you like kids," I said.

Whit scowled again. "Kids are honest. They don't snow you."

I didn't know how to respond to that. I didn't have to, because Racine said, "Ashley, I want to ask you something. I haven't made any progress being Racine Wisconsin. How do you like 'Meg Benedict'?"

"Over easy, with a pinch of salt," I said.

Whit laughed, and for the rest of the trip his face was relaxed.

It wasn't very far to the river. As Abel had said the first day, it was just over George Hill. Whit drove carefully down a steep road dug into the hillside, and we were there.

The river wound through a narrow valley, which it had probably dug for itself through the eons of time. Cottonwood trees and chokecherry bushes grew along its edges, and the bank where we stopped was grassy.

About thirty people were milling around. Some of them held inflated innertubes. Most of the people were teenagers, but there were about five adults who must have been the Mutual advisers. A blond guy was handing out innertubes from the back of a truck.

"Hey, Whit, Racine," he yelled. "Come get your tubes." He gave me a friendly grin. "We brought one for you too, Ashley."

I looked at Racine. "How does he know my name?"

She shrugged. "Psychic maybe?" She gave my arm a little punch. "Word gets around in a little town like this. I guess somebody told him."

And that's probably how Gideon had known my name.

Somebody told him. Abel? Abel knew all about the story of Gideon and George. And he hadn't seemed surprised when I told him I'd seen a guy who said he was a ghost. Had Abel talked with him?

I put the thought aside. I'd think about it later.

One of the guys ran toward the river. "Last one in's a rotten egg." He splashed into the water up to his knees.

"Now hold on a minute," yelled one of the adult men. "Let's establish a few rules. No one goes shooting off alone, right? We stay together. I don't want to be dragging any soggy bodies home to your folks."

Everybody agreed and went for the water.

"Is innertubing dangerous?" I asked Whit.

He shrugged. "Depends on you. The river has a bad reputation, but it's safe enough if you don't get reckless. A few people have drowned here, but not while innertubing."

"Remember George Glessing that we were talking about the other day?" Racine said. "This is where he drowned. Right there, out in the middle."

I looked across the smooth, dark surface of the river. The water slid quietly between its banks.

"Right here? It doesn't look that menacing."

Whit scowled again and I knew I was sounding like a city girl.

"You can't see the currents," he said. He spoke as if explaining to a dense little kid, and I knew I'd lost ground.

Not that I cared.

The trick about innertubing was to get into the tube in the first place. Whit and Racine showed me how to steady it with one hand while I backed up to it and tried to sit in the center.

But the current snatched the tube, and when I sat, there was only water to catch me. My tube went whirling off on its own.

Whit went after it. "See what I mean?" he said when he brought it back to me. "The currents are there."

This time he held it steady while I jackknifed myself into it, legs dangling over one side and arms hanging from the other.

The current took both me and the tube, spinning us downstream. It was safe enough, I told myself, as long as I didn't struggle or try to get out of the tube.

"Paddle with your hands," Whit called. "Find a gentler current." He got into his own tube and came after me.

I paddled, working at staying calm.

"Over here," Whit said, bobbing like a rubber duck.

I paddled harder, and when I got near enough, he reached out a hand to take mine. His hand was wide and strong, and I was immensely grateful for it.

"Scared?" he asked.

"Yeah." It was all I could say for a minute. "But I love it." I did. It was the kind of danger Richard craved, where you could be wiped out if you didn't keep your head. He'd trained me to think in tight places. That was something Mom and Dad didn't understand. "You were right about the currents. Thanks for helping me."

Whit didn't let go of my hand. "You're pretty gutsy, Ashley," he said. "Some people panic when the current grabs them."

I'd regained a point.

Everybody was launched by now, and I saw several people hooking up the way Whit and I were. Racine paddled over and took Whit's other hand so we could travel together.

"It's fast today," she said. "I wonder if they're letting water through the dam."

I looked ahead, downriver. "There's a dam?"

"Yes," Whit said. "It's about five miles ahead. There's a power station. We always check when we're going tubing because if they let a lot of water through, it's too dangerous to go out."

I thought about it. "Is that what happened when George Glessing drowned?"

"He drowned years before the power station was built," Whit said. "I guess he just wasn't a good enough swimmer to get all the way across."

I looked at the river and thought of Gideon frantically diving into the dark water, looking for his brother. And realizing it was his fault that George was dead.

For the first time I began to understand how Gideon must have felt. I still didn't know how ghosts could make footprints, but how could I deny that the horror of what had happened might be strong enough to keep Gideon wandering the earth, calling for George.

I wanted to see him again, to comfort him and tell him I understood.

And ask him about the danger he saw in my own future.

Chapter Seven

For a while I forgot about Gideon and even Richard. Once I got the hang of tubing, I relaxed and enjoyed it. The river wasn't anything like the ocean I loved, except that it was cold and wet. But it had its own delights.

There were those unseen fast currents that spun us dizzily around, tearing my hand from Whit's so that he and I and Racine all floated freely. Then there were calm spots where all thirty of us linked hands and drifted lazily, like a long, slow train, under the overhanging willow and chokecherry bushes.

That's when the others asked me questions.

"What's it like to surf?" a guy called Laser asked.

"Don't know," I told him. "I'm not a surfer."

"I thought all Californians were surfers. What's your best thing, then?"

"I'm good at lying on the sand." I sprawled back on my tube to show how good I was at it.

"I could do that," said a girl named Tanya. "When are you going down there again?"

"Soon."

"You got a guy there?" Tanya asked.

"Yes. Yes, I do."

I saw Whit glance at me. I couldn't read his look.

It didn't matter. I knew he liked me a lot better than he had before. But he might as well know right off that I was interested in somebody else. That way he wouldn't have a replay of last summer when the girl from Phoenix dumped him and he came all unglued.

We tubed for about three miles, then paddled to shore. Somebody had gone ahead and built a fire for a wiener roast. There was a lot of laughter and talk as we charred the franks and slathered them with mustard.

The sun disappeared behind the western ridge of the narrow little valley as we ate. Darkness deepened the shadows under the tall trees and drooping bushes. The river muttered softly and a night wind whispered down through the canyon. It was a time for ghost stories.

"Hey, you guys," Tanya said, "don't you think we ought to initiate Ashley?"

"Here?"

I couldn't see who said that.

"Sure," Tanya said, "It's almost as creepy here as it is at the old house."

"No way," Whit said. "If we're going to initiate her, let's do it right."

I wondered if he would have said that if I hadn't told them I had a guy in California. Was he getting back at me for what that other girl had done to him?

"She's already been up to the old house," Racine said. "Alone. I think that's enough initiation."

I held my breath, waiting for her to tell them I'd seen Gideon.

She didn't. She looked at me, and in the firelight I saw her wink.

"What's the big deal?" I said. "It's just another broken-down old house. I've seen a hundred old houses."

Laser laughed. "Not like this one."

What could be different about that old house? I remembered it, dark and gloomy under the tall trees.

"When are we going to do the initiation?" the girl named Tanya asked.

"How about Monday night," Laser said. "Let's meet at the old schoolhouse at ten. We'll pick up Ashley on the way and get things going as soon as it's dark."

On the way home I asked Racine if she'd told me all there was to know about the initiation. She shrugged. "As far as I know. I didn't go to the last one."

"It's just a bunch of corny spook stuff," Whit said as he steered the car up the narrow, rocky ledge of a road. "Some of the juvenile types like to think it's scary."

"Hey," I said, "who was it that insisted it should be done up at the old house?"

Whit grinned. "As I said, some of *us* juvenile types like it."

"How come your folks allow you juvenile types to wander around haunted houses late at night?" I was wondering if my own parents would let me go.

"Who do you think started these initiation rites?" Whit asked. "It's been a tradition for a long, long time. If your folks object, Mom will call and tell them it's okay."

It didn't sound like any big deal.

When we got to the McFadden house, we saw a string of Christmas lights flashing on the little tree by the gate.

"That means we're supposed to stop," Racine said. "It's one of Mom's signals."

Whit pulled to a stop. "She has a signal for every occasion."

"You might as well come in too, Ashley." Whit slid out and extended a hand for me. "This might concern you."

"Me?" My heart lurched. Had something happened to my family while I'd been gone? Was that what Gideon had meant about my future being trashed?

Racine laughed. "Don't look so worried. Your brothers seemed pretty gung ho about coming over to meet the troops. They're probably here and want to go home."

They were there, all right, but they didn't want to go home. They were lost in the swarm of young McFaddens and seemed supremely happy.

"I told your mother they could stay until you kids came home from the party," Mrs. McFadden explained.

It took a while to separate them from the McFaddens. We had to cut them out like a couple of calves from a herd of cattle.

"Ashley," Truman said, "have you ever been in a treehouse?"

"They've got a cave." Finn's eyes glazed over with awe. "It's right there in the side of the hill."

"I wish I could live here," Truman whispered.

"We have to go home," I said.

I wished Finn and Truman had never discovered the McFaddens. They hadn't had many friends in our neighborhood in California, and this was just one more thing to nail us to this little town.

"They've got ten cats and more horses than I can count and a goose named Honk." Truman wasn't about to be turned off.

"I hope they haven't been too much trouble," I said.

Mrs. McFadden smiled. She looked tired. "What's a couple more? How was your party?"

"Good," Whit said. "We're going to have another one Monday night when we initiate Ashley."

"One of our small-town customs," Mrs. McFadden said. "Don't worry about it, Ashley."

"Hey, guys, let's go." Whit began herding Finn and Truman toward the door. Racine held back the swarm of young McFaddens, all of whom wanted to go with us.

Behind Whit's back, Mrs. McFadden caught my eye. Her lips formed words, but I couldn't tell what they were. I frowned, indicating I didn't understand.

Mrs. McFadden drifted toward me. "Goodnight, boys," she sang out after Finn and Truman. "Come again soon."

They went out, followed by Whit and Racine.

I was leaving, too, when Mrs. McFadden touched my arm.

"Warn Gideon," she said in my ear.

Before I could give her a puzzled look, Racine swooped back, linking her arm in mine. "Bring the boys over after church tomorrow," she said, "and we'll talk about guys."

Warn Gideon. The words rattled around in my head all night long. Why did he need to be warned, and about what? If these initiation trips to the old house were a regular thing, then he must be expecting this one. If he really was a ghost, the way he kept insisting, then wouldn't he know without my telling him that a crowd was coming?

One thing was certain. Mrs. McFadden knew a lot more about him than either Whit or Racine did.

*   *   *

I didn't go back to the McFaddens' the next day because Mrs. McFadden went to the hospital that night. I learned about it on the steps of the church the next morning.

"But she hasn't had the baby yet," Racine said. She was juggling Fuffer and and Petey John, and I noticed Whit was herding the other kids. "We'll probably have our new sister by this afternoon."

"Or brother," I suggested.

"It'll be a girl. Remember what I said about patterns?" Racine grabbed for a handful of Petey John's sparkling white shirt as he made a sudden bolt back down the stairs. "Come on, P. J.," she coaxed, "I'll take you to your class."

"I want Mom to do it," he said.

"She's at the hospital," Racine said patiently. "She's getting a new baby."

"She already has a new baby." Petey John pointed at Fuffer. "What's she need another one for?"

"She loves babies. We all do, P. J. Just wait'll she brings our new sister home."

Petey John tried to pull away. "Where's she gonna put it?" he demanded. "She holds Fuffer with one arm and me with the other. She doesn't have any more arms for a new baby."

Racine looked up at me. "Trouble," she said. "We can finish this discussion when you come to my house after church."

"Racine, I don't think I should come. You'll have your hands full, taking care of the kids."

Racine shrugged. "So what's new?"

Petey John yanked away and took off.

"Let me take Fuffer," I said, and Racine thrust him at me. "I'll come over another day," I said over the top of his head. "I have something else I have to do today."

In fact, I had two things I wanted to do. I wanted to warn Gideon that day so he'd have plenty of time to hide. But the first thing was to call Richard. As soon as I got home, I dialed his number on the telephone.

"Hello?" He answered so fast that he must have been standing there with his hand on his phone.

"Richard! Hi! It's me."

"Ashley!" I could hear the pleasure flood his voice. "Where are you calling from? Are you back here in Pasadena?"

"Oh, I wish I were. No, I'm calling from the wilds of Idaho."

He gave a little groan. "I wish you were here. Things are grim without you."

My heart did a fast tap dance. "How grim?"

"We spent a lot of time talking about you at the beach party last night. Everybody misses you."

"Who's we?"

"Val and Eddie were there. And Monique. She asked about you."

I'll bet she did!

"And Mary Lyn and Diane and Roz."

I began to feel a little like Petey John. With all those girls around, did Richard have any arms left for me?

"Richard, I've had a great idea. Why don't you come up here? To Idaho? You could finish your last year of school here, and we could be together."

He was silent for a moment and I was afraid I'd said too much. Then he said, "I hadn't thought of that. But I *was* thinking I'd come up to see you. We can talk about your idea when I get there."

I couldn't believe my ears. "Really? Are you really coming?"

He laughed. "Really! Didn't I tell you how much I miss you? Just as soon as I can get somebody to substitute for me at the hardware store, I'll be there."

That worried me a little. "Can you take off from your job, Richard? Will they let you do that?" I remembered how happy he'd been to get that summer job so he could buy his own gas and bullets and all the other things he needed.

"When I tell them I'm going to see the prettiest girl in the world, they'll be glad to give me time off." He laughed again. "Hey, honey-babe, I can't wait. I'll bring my motorcycle along so we can try out those mountains you wrote about. Are there bike trails?"

"If there aren't, we'll make some," I said breathlessly. "And you can check out jobs around here. And . . . Richard? If you don't like it here, then maybe my folks would let me go back to California with you. Val says I could live with her family."

"There's another option open," Richard said, and I knew he meant marrying him.

But that was too heavy to think about right then.

"I'll see you soon," Richard said as he hung up.

I was beyond Cloud Nine as I went to the corral to saddle Skyrocket for my trip to warn Gideon.

Abel was there at the corral, feeding the animals.

"Good news?" he asked.

"How can you tell?"

"Your face. Don't need the sun, it's shining so bright."

I laughed joyously. "Richard's coming, Abel. My guy from California. He's coming up here to see me."

"Your folks know?" He sounded disapproving.

Like Gideon.

Suddenly things began to add up. All those things that Gideon knew about me — Abel must have told him. Which meant that Gideon wasn't a ghost with supernatural powers. But why would Abel tell him about me? What did Abel have to do with him in the first place? And Mrs. McFadden. What did she know about Gideon?

I felt unseen currents, as dark and mysterious as those in the river, swirling about me.

Chapter Eight

"Abel," I said, "you know all about Gideon up there at the old house, don't you." It was a statement, not a question, and Abel didn't deny it.

"He scare you?" he asked.

"No. Well, maybe, because I don't know what to make of him. Is he really a ghost?"

"What's *he* say about it?"

"He says he is."

"Hate to call a feller a liar."

I flapped my arms in exasperation. "But there are no such things as ghosts. Besides, he makes footprints."

Abel shrugged. "Never have been right chummy with a ghost. Don't know if they make footprints or not."

I wasn't getting anywhere with him.

"I came out to get Skyrocket," I said. "I'm going up to the old house." I thought a second, then decided to tell him everything. "A bunch of guys and girls are going up there tomorrow night. They're going to initiate me into full citizenship in Blue Creek."

Abel stiffened a little and glanced up the canyon where the creeks meet. But all he said was, "Seems like the young folks have always liked to do that. Better'n watching TV, I reckon."

I scuffed a foot in the dirt by the corral. "Mrs. Mc-Fadden said I should warn Gideon. I'm going up there now to do that."

Abel relaxed. "Right thoughty of you. He'd appreciate knowing."

"Doesn't he already know? If he's a ghost, wouldn't he know without my telling him?"

Abel shook his head. "Don't rightly know."

"Aren't ghosts supposed to know these things? Abel, did you tell Gideon about my plans to go to California? And my name?"

"I wouldn't do that, Ashley. Told you before, I don't tell secrets."

The way he stood let me know he was offended.

"Sorry. I'm just a little confused, that's all."

Confused wasn't exactly the right word. Perplexed would be better. Or stunned. Scared stiff would be best, because if Abel hadn't told Gideon, how did he find out?

Was it possible he really *was* a ghost?

This time I guided Skyrocket well away from the swamp. I didn't want any replays of previous adventures.

"Gideon," I called as soon as I came within hearing distance of the house. "Gideon, I need to talk with you."

Sunlight glinted off the one pane of glass left in the old dormer window. The leaves of the quaking aspen shivered and a small, fat animal scampered into the trees.

"Gideon?"

I whoaed Skyrocked to a stop and searched the clearing with my eyes. I wanted to see how Gideon came, whether he walked into my sight or just materialized.

"GIDEON!"

I could hear my heart thudding in my chest. Skyrocket moved his big feet, making rustling sounds in the dry weeds.

What was I doing there anyway? Why didn't I just tell Whit and the others I didn't want to be initiated? Richard was coming. Maybe we'd be going back to California soon, so I didn't need to become a citizen of Blue Creek. What did it matter if Racine and Whit and the others thought I was a poor sport?

I kicked Skyrocket's sides and turned him around. But then I pulled him to a stop. I didn't want to leave actually believing in ghosts. If I went into the old house and looked around, I might find some clue that Gideon was a flesh-and-blood guy. There might be a sleeping bag there, or some evidence of food.

Skyrocket patiently obeyed my urging to turn again toward the house. I rode up close and got off, tying him to a cottonwood tree and knotting the bridle rein firmly, as Whit had taught me.

The porch steps groaned as I stepped on them, and I wondered if the old wood might be rotten. Was there a cellar beneath the house that I would plunge into if the floor gave way? Were there snakes down there?

Treading carefully, I walked into what must have been the kitchen. It was totally empty except for the dust and broken planks and a length of rusted stovepipe. Plaster had fallen from the walls, revealing the skeleton of the house. I peered behind some of the decaying boards to see if anything could be hidden inside the walls.

But I found nothing. Not in the kitchen nor in the bedroom nor in the tiny lean-to that could have been another bedroom or maybe a pantry or closet.

There was no sign at all that anybody was living there.

"Okay," I said aloud, "so that's that." And I turned to see Gideon standing in the doorway. A shaft of sunlight coming from behind made an aura around him.

"Gideon!" I gasped. "Couldn't you give me some warning?"

Those white teeth of his flashed and he said, "Section two, paragraph six of the *Handbook of Ghosting* states that surprise is a major element of haunting."

His teasing made me angry, which was good because the anger overcame my fright.

"I came up here to do you a favor," I huffed, "and now you're making fun of me."

"Sorry." He moved into the shadowy room.

"Why didn't you come when I called?" I demanded. "I almost yelled myself hoarse."

"I didn't hear you. I was out in the woods watching a gopher build his home. Have you ever seen a gopher dig a burrow, Ashley?"

"Good grief, no," I said. "When we get gophers in our lawn at home, we poison them."

"You wouldn't believe how they push the dirt out, particle by particle." Gideon gazed out of the window. "Would you like to see it?"

"No, but I *would* like to go outside. This place gives me the creeps."

I expected him to make some teasing remark about that, but he merely turned and led the way outside.

"I'm glad you came," he said. "There's something I've been wanting to show you." He walked toward a little path that swung off under the cottonwoods and quaking aspen. "Let's walk to the top of the hill, and you can tell me why you came."

"I came to warn you." I had to run to keep up with him. "A lot of the kids in town are coming up here to-morrow night. It's to be an initiation for me."

"Thanks for the warning." His high, laced boots crunched on the rocky path.

"Mrs. McFadden told me to warn you." I was begin-ning to puff. "She's in the hospital. They think she might have the baby today."

"Yes." He nodded his head. "Yes, I know that."

How did he know?

Gideon continued to talk, but so softly that I couldn't hear.

"What did you say?" I asked.

He turned his head slightly. "I said Mrs. McFadden knows about the past and the future."

"I don't know what you mean," I panted. The steep path was rutted and full of rocks. I had to watch where I put my feet. If I fell, I knew I wouldn't get any help from Gideon.

"The present is the print-out of all the input from the past," he said, almost as if to himself. "It's only the future that we can program."

"Since when," I puffed, "do ghosts know computer-speak?"

Gideon stopped racing up the hill and turned to grin at me. "I told you, ghosts know all. Remember?"

I stopped, too, and leaned over with my hands on my knees. "How come you didn't know about the initiation tomorrow night then?"

"How do you know I didn't know?"

Why was I running up the hill with someone who frustrated me as much as Gideon did?

"I'm going back," I said.

"No," he said. "We're almost to the top. I'm going to show you something."

"The gopher building his home?"

He smiled. "No. Something else."

He started up again, and I toiled after him, right to the top of George Hill.

On the other side was the narrow little valley with Bear River flowing through it. I could see where we'd gone innertubing the day before.

After I'd caught my breath, Gideon motioned for me to climb up on a large, flat-topped rock.

"Now," he said, "here's what I want you to see. Look back there where the creeks meet."

Far down the hill I saw the old house and the V where the creeks flowed together.

"Now, follow the main stream down a few miles and see where several other creeks flow into it. Beyond that peak, the creek flows into the river. Several miles farther on, that river meets another river, and that one meets another. They keep flowing together, getting bigger and bigger, until they eventually flow into the sea."

"Did I climb all the way up here for a geography lesson?" I asked. It wasn't anything new. I'd thought of the same thing when I first came up to where the creeks meet.

Gideon was gazing off into the distance. "Doesn't this flowing together mean anything to you? How can you separate one drop of water from another? Where does one end and another begin? How can I separate my life from all those others?"

Now I knew what he was getting at. It was a continuation of the lecture he'd started before, about people's lives influencing other people's lives. Bringing me up to the top of the mountain was just a visual aid.

"I get the point," I said.

But Gideon went on talking, his speech rapid and force-ful although his voice was soft. He was looking down at the river now.

"It's *my* life," he said. "*My* trip. But the creeks flow together. The water . . . the water . . . swim! Don't sink! It's muddy down there. I can't see. Robbie! Where are the lights? The creeks flow together. Like the blood. Robbie! Robbie!"

"Gideon," I said. "What's the matter?"

His eyes passed over me but weren't focusing. "Mrs. McFadden knows. The past flows into the present, and you drag the chains into the future, unless . . . unless . . ."

He was pacing back and forth now, staring down at the river.

For one terrified moment I considered running, bolting back to the safety and sanity of our house, back to Mother. But I couldn't leave anyone, not even a despairing ghost, alone on a mountaintop in Gideon's condition.

"Gideon," I said, "let me take you to my mother. She's a counselor. She can help you."

He shook his head violently. "No. No help. It's done. It's happened. It can't unhappen. I'll show you. He's bur-ied down there in the cemetery. I can show you. They said it wasn't my fault. But I know. I know."

"George?" I said. "Your brother George?"

"Yes. He always wanted to do what I did. The lights! The lights!"

I made a move to take hold of Gideon's arm, ghost or no ghost, but he backed out of my reach.

"Gideon," I said, "who is Robbie? You said Robbie before."

"Robbie?" He stared at me. "Robbie?"

I could see his eyes focusing again. "Did I say Robbie?"

"Is Robbie your brother, too?"

"No." He shook his head. "No." He drew a deep, quavering breath. "Ashley, I'm so sorry. I didn't mean to flip out on you like that. I wouldn't have brought you up here if I'd known I was going to do that."

"You need help, Gideon," I said. "If you won't let my mother help you, then go to Mrs. McFadden."

He shook his head again. "No. Mrs. McFadden . . ." He paused, then said, "Mrs. McFadden wanted you to warn me so I can stay out of the way tomorrow night. Let me sit here on the rock for a minute, then we'll go back down." He sat down. "Don't worry about the initiation. I'll be all right."

"Are you sure, Gideon? I could call them off, you know, then you wouldn't have to hide. I don't need to be initiated. I'll probably be leaving Blue Creek this week anyway. Richard is coming. He's my guy. I'll probably be going back to California with him."

"Go ahead with the initiation." He stood up. "You might as well be an official citizen of Blue Creek. If you go back to California with Richard, it will be over my dead body." He smiled broadly at me and started down the hill.

He was teasing me again.

Or was he?

Chapter Nine

I must have looked as washed out as I felt when I got home because Mom said, "Ashley, what happened?"

She was sitting at the dining room table, writing letters. Dad was taking a nap in his favorite chair in the living room, and I could hear Finn and Truman playing outside on the lawn.

I drooped onto a chair and picked up a pen lying on the table beside it. What I really wanted to do was crawl into Mom's lap the way I used to do when I was a little kid. I wanted to tell her all my hurts and let her kiss them better.

But it wasn't I who was hurt. It was Gideon. And he didn't want help.

"I've been riding, Mom." I scrubbed at my sweaty face and pushed back my hair. "I forgot to take a hat. It's hot out there."

Mom reached over and took the pen from me. "It leaks," she said. "Now you've got ink all over your face."

Oh well. It was that kind of a day. I wondered how I could get Mom's help without actually telling her about Gideon. Maybe I could use the old thing about, "A friend has this problem . . ." But how many of my friends thought they were ghosts? How do you ask about something like that?

"Richard called," Mom said.

"Richard?" I'd been so concerned with Gideon that I'd forgotten about Richard.

Mom gave me a small smile. "Richard. You know, the guy with the red truck."

"What did he say?"

"He said, 'Tell Ashley all systems are go.' "

All systems are go! That must mean he was on his way. If I could just hang on for a couple more days, he'd come and carry me off, like the prince in the fairy tales.

"Did he say when he'd get here?" I asked.

Mom stopped writing and turned to look at me. "Is he coming here?"

"I guess I forgot to mention it."

"That's pretty important stuff to forget about. I thought we left that whole Richard problem behind."

We were back to the old argument. "You took me away from him, Mom. I didn't leave him behind. *You* did."

"Ashley, he's just not the kind of boy . . ." She stopped and was silent for a moment. "How long's he going to stay?"

I certainly wasn't going to tell her yet that when he left, I'd be going with him.

When the telephone rang, I thought it would be Richard again. But it was Racine.

"Hi," she said cheerfully. "Ready for the initiation tomorrow night?"

"Racine," I said, "this is really kid stuff." I wondered how Gideon was going to stay out of the way. Would he go back to the mountaintop and maybe flip out again, all alone there in the darkness? "Can't we call it off?"

"No way. We don't have a whole lot of entertainment around here, and we never pass up an opportunity like this. I just called to say there isn't anything to be scared of. It's just a lot of fooling around."

"What exactly do you mean by fooling around?"

"Oh, moans and chains rattling and all that. They'll put on quite a show for you. We've had a couple of girls almost get hysterical, but other than that there hasn't been any damage to anybody. If you want to act real scared, it'll make them happy and they'll probably end it sooner."

"Thanks for telling me. I'll scream up a storm."

"Good. See you soon."

Before she hung up, I said, "Racine, how's your mother? Has that new sister arrived yet?"

"Not yet," she said. "Dad just came home. He says it's probably a false alarm, but they want to keep Mom at the hospital for a little while. This gives me more time to figure out the right name for the baby. What do you think of Scarlett O'Hara McFadden?"

"Well, the Scarlett O'Hara part has been done."

"That's the point, Ashley. If we name her Scarlett O'Hara, then she'll have a life full of romance and Rhett Butlers. Remember my theory about the past recycling if you just get the right pattern going?"

I laughed. "Scarlett O'Hara isn't the past, ninny. She's fiction. Somebody made her up."

Racine sighed. "Killjoy. Well, maybe we'll call her Princess Di or something. Maybe she can snag a prince."

"Why don't you just let her live her own life?" I suggested. "You've got her life all mapped out before she's even born. And what if she's a he?"

"She won't be," Racine said cheerfully. "I'll see you tomorrow night."

Racine was so naive. She thought a name could make a difference in a person's life.

There were clouds in front of the moon on Monday night. It was a perfect night for a trip to a haunted house, if you were just going for the fun of it.

Whit and Racine and Laser and five other kids came for me in the old battered blue van. Everybody moved over to make a space for me.

Mom and Dad watched from the doorway. They had checked out initiations with some other people in town, and Dad said he thought it sounded like fun.

Finn thought it did too.

"Can I go?" he yelled from the doorway.

He was dressed in his pajamas.

"In four or five years," Whit called back. "Then it'll be your turn."

"*Nobody* ever wants me along," Finn complained.

Whit started the engine and we rattled off across the stone bridge and up the rutted road to the old house. The van couldn't make it all the way, so we had that long hike to do. Several people had flashlights, but the footing on the rocky trail was still precarious and I stumbled. Whit walked behind me and reached up to steady me when I needed it.

"Thanks," I said, "I'm not used to night hikes."

"You're doing fine," Whit said. "You could have said no to this whole thing, you know."

"*Now* you tell me. I didn't know I had a choice."

Whit chuckled. "You always have a choice. But everybody likes you better if you go along with the fun."

I looked ahead at a couple of the guys who carried gunnysacks filled with something. Props for the production, probably. Who knew what they were going to do?

"I *hope* it's fun," I said, skidding on a rock.

I felt Whit's steadying hand on my arm. "Look, I'll take care of you. Don't worry about it."

I was more worried about Gideon than I was about me. I hoped he'd stay out of sight.

We could barely see the outline of the old house in the dim light of the moon. It sort of hung there in the darkness under the big cottonwoods. Everybody had been laughing and talking on the trail, but now they fell silent. I don't know if that was the plan or if that was how the place affected them.

An animal cried from the direction of the swamp, and I wondered if it was stuck in the slime.

Or was it one of the guys providing sound effects?

Laser seemed to be the leader of the group. He stepped up on the sagging old porch. "You have to leave your flashlights outside," he announced. "We use only candlelight inside."

He held up a tall white candle stuck in the neck of a 7-Up bottle, then took a match from his pocket and lit it. He held the candle high while everyone deposited flashlights on the porch, like cowboys checking their weapons outside a saloon in a western movie. Then we all went inside, walking carefully across the creaking floorboards of the old kitchen.

Laser set the candle down in the middle of the room. "Form a circle around it," he said. "Sit close enough to hold hands when the time comes."

When what time came? I glanced uneasily into the shadowy corners of the room.

Everyone sat down on the dirty floor. The dim light of the candle made their faces look white and bloated, with caverns for eyes.

"First we'll tell you the story of Gideon," Laser said. "We never quite know what will happen, Ashley, so you'd better hold hands with the people on either side of you."

I felt Whit's hand, big and warm, reach out for my left hand. I put out my right hand toward Racine, and my fingers closed on something icy and hard, like cold bones.

I screamed. I couldn't help it. I hadn't expected the tricks to start yet.

The candle suddenly went out, as if a door had opened somewhere and a wind blew in.

"It's just a plastic skeleton's hand," Racine whispered in the darkness. "I've had it in an insulated bag of ice all the way up here. We always use it."

There was some shuffling, then Laser said, "I can't get the candle lit again. Are you here, Gideon?"

Silence.

"Sometimes he does that," Laser intoned. "He doesn't like the light."

I suspected this was all part of the set-up.

"Gideon?" Laser said. "Do you want to tell your own story?"

More silence.

"All right. Then Keith will tell it."

The guy named Keith cleared his throat. "The story begins many, many years ago when two little brothers played happily in this very spot. Right in this room."

Keith's voice was low and husky. He must have had some drama classes, because he knew how to tell a story.

"Gideon was the daring one," Keith went on. "But little brother Georgie didn't want to be left out. 'Let me go with you,' Georgie said every time Gideon went any-where."

Like Finn. I could imagine little Georgie in his tattered pajamas standing in the doorway, pleading to go along.

The quiet voice went on in the darkness, telling how Gideon rode high-spirited horses and Georgie tried to do the same, only to be bucked off. Keith told of Gideon daring to walk through the swamp, and Georgie getting bogged down in the middle.

Somewhere in the darkness a high-pitched, eerie tune began to play. There must have been a tape recorder in one of the gunnysacks.

Keith's voice picked up in volume and intensity. He told of Gideon and Georgie's teenage years. I wondered if he was making it all up or if he'd done research on it.

"In the cemetery," he went on, "is a headstone with the name of George Glessing on it, and a date—July 7, 1909. And this is what happened on that awful day."

There was a faint glow in one corner of the room. It grew a little brighter, and I could see that it was shaped like a headstone, white with black lettering on it.

Good touch, I thought. It had to be battery-operated and someone turned it on at the right moment.

Keith was speaking rapidly. "It started out as a happy family picnic. Their mother had fried a couple of chickens and made a cream cake. Everyone was full and sleepy, except for Gideon and Georgie."

Suddenly a figure rose from behind the tombstone. "I dared George to follow me into the water," the voice whis-pered. "I thought he'd back out."

Gideon? Again I screamed involuntarily. The guy was dressed in a short jacket and a billed cap similar to the one Gideon always wore.

But it wasn't Gideon's voice that was whispering those terrible words. It was somebody else, playing a part.

"I dived again and again, searching those dark waters for George," the voice continued. "My lungs were bursting, but I dived to the bottom, groping among the rocks and dirt for my brother."

I wanted to scream for the voice to stop. This was all wrong, to use someone's pain for entertainment. Even if that person was dead now too, it was wrong. Poor Gideon.

I didn't get a chance to say anything, because something whammed into the side of the house, startling everybody.

"No!" a voice said. "He's not dead. Look! He's just pretending. George! Wake up!"

This time it *was* Gideon's voice.

"Hey, what's going on?" That was Laser.

I heard people getting to their feet in the darkness.

"Somebody give me the candle," Laser said.

Whit let go of my hand and scrambled to the center of the circle. "I can't find it," he said. "What's happened to it?"

"Go for the flashlights," Laser said tensely. "Somebody's horning in on this."

Gideon's voice went on. "In the mud. There's no lights. Robbie! Robbie!"

People bumped into me in the murky light from the tombstone. I didn't dare move. I didn't know which way to go. The darkness had disoriented me.

"Ashley!" That was Whit. "Stay in here. I'll come get you as soon as I find a light."

There was a splintering sound, and a girl screamed. "My foot went through the floor," she said. "Help me!"

I couldn't hear Gideon talking anymore. I hoped he'd

already run off into the woods. But he'd sounded as if he were reliving the past. Would he think of running? What would happen if they caught him?

Or was it all part of the show?

I got to my feet and stood uncertainly in the darkness. I had to get out of there. I was losing reality.

Then someone was beside me.

"This way," a male voice whispered.

I stumbled and he swooped me up into his arms. Good, solid, flesh-and-blood arms.

"Whit," I said, "I'm so glad you came."

"It's not Whit, Robbie," he whispered in my ear. "It's Gideon."

Chapter Ten

"Gideon," I gasped. "Put me down."

He was walking carefully through the darkness of the old kitchen.

"I'll take care of you, Robbie. You're going to be all right. It won't be like the other time."

I could feel puffs of air on my ear as he spoke.

"Gideon!" I tried to firm up my voice so it wouldn't shake. "Gideon, *I'm not Robbie*. Listen to me. I'm *Ashley*. Please put me down."

We were outside by then, but it was still pitch black. A slight breeze made the trees whisper around us.

"Ashley?" Gideon sounded puzzled.

"Yes. I'm Ashley. Your new friend, Ashley. You saved me from the swamp."

Gideon stopped, and I could feel him take a deep breath. He took in so much air I thought he'd burst, like an overfilled balloon.

Then he let it out with a whoosh. "Ashley. I'm sorry. I guess it's flip-out time again."

From the front of the house I could hear shouting. Whit called, "Ashley, are you all right?"

"Has anybody found a flashlight yet?" Laser asked.

"Gideon," I said once more, "let me down."

He set me down in the darkness, then took my hand.

"Let's go over under the cottonwoods where they won't see us."

I pulled back. "I have to go back to them. They'll be looking all over for me."

"In a minute."

I had no choice but to follow him. I didn't know where we were in relation to the house, and I didn't have the strength to resist his tugging hand. When he finally stopped, I heard leaves rattle over our heads.

"I didn't mean for it to happen that way," Gideon said. "I mean my weirding out like that. I was just going to have a little fun with those guys. Haunt them a little. After all, they came here looking for a ghost."

My heartbeat slowed a little and I could think again. "Gideon, you're no ghost. Ghosts don't breathe and have warm hands and smell of aftershave lotion."

"Depends on your definition of a ghost, Ashley."

Whit's voice at the front of the house was getting frantic as he called for me. Through the trees I saw a glow and knew somebody had found the flashlights.

"I've got to go now. But give me at least one straight answer before I do, Gideon. Who is Robbie?"

He didn't say anything.

"Did something happen to Robbie? Is that why you're hiding here?"

There was a light at the back of the house now. In a minute Whit would be looking under the trees for me.

"Secrets, Ashley," Gideon said. "I told you that first day that I had secrets." I could tell by his voice that he'd taken a few steps away from me. "You'd better go now."

"I want to help you."

"Nobody can help me."

"Our lives flow together, Gideon. Remember? You told me that up on the mountain. My life has flowed into yours. Let me help you."

"Meet me tomorrow." He was getting farther away.

"Here?"

"In the cemetery. By my grave. Five o'clock."

"Ashley!"

That was Whit. He was getting closer, and I could see his light along the path.

"I'm here, Whit." I headed toward the light but stumbled over a root. I heard Gideon's soft footsteps as he swooped back to help me to my feet. Then, without a word, he took my face between his hands and kissed me softly on the lips, a sweet, unbelievably tender kiss.

Still without saying anything, he was gone.

Whit scolded me all the way down the trail.

"Why did you leave the house? I told you I'd come after you. Why didn't you wait?" He sounded like a nagging parent.

"It was scary in there." That was the truth.

"Wasn't it scarier out in the trees?"

"I didn't know where I was going." That was the truth, too.

"Leave her alone, Whit," Racine said in my defense. "She's had enough for tonight."

"Sorry," Whit apologized. "It's just that I got really scared about you."

"Oh, I forgot," I said sarcastically. "*I* was supposed to be the only one to get scared."

"Well, it was a dumb thing to do, running off into the trees like that."

"Let it be, Whit," Racine said firmly. "Who do you think whammed on the house and acted like Gideon?"

"I don't know." Whit's voice was grumpy.

Racine giggled. "Maybe it was really Gideon."

Whit evidently didn't think that was worth considering. "It was some of the guys who said they weren't coming up here with us. They probably sneaked up early and hid so they could scare us."

"I prefer to think it was Gideon," Racine said. "How about you, Ashley. Do you think it was a ghost?"

"It depends on your definition of a ghost," I told her, remembering what Gideon had said.

My journal entry that night was "I was kissed by a ghost." That ought to thrill my great-grandchildren someday. Would the story of Gideon survive that long? Would the old house still be there? Would the Gideon I knew still haunt the hills, crying out for Robbie, even though he wasn't a ghost?

I looked at my journal entry again, wondering if I should cross it out. Letting it stay would just preserve the old legend of Gideon's ghost, like the story in Racine's great-grandfather's diary. Had he really seen something that day when he was cutting trees? Could it have been a shadow, as Gideon said? Or had the conk on his head made him think something was there? Was the story of the ghost just something that had started with a young man's troubles many years ago and then was built upon by people who were spooked by the old house down through the years? Had it been built up so strongly that it had affected the present-day Gideon—if that was indeed his name?

Was that what he meant by lives flowing together?

I closed my journal. I would write the truth in when

I found out what it was. Maybe that would be as soon as the next afternoon, when I kept the rendezvous with Gideon in the cemetery.

Richard called early the next morning.

"I'm on my way, Ashley." He sounded excited. "I chucked my job and I'm splitting this whole scene."

My heart raced. "Does that mean you're going to stay here in Blue Creek?"

He laughed. "I've got something to talk over with you. I'll tell you then."

"Tell me now, Richard. I can't wait."

"Hang on. I'll be there tomorrow night."

He wasn't going to tell. "Drive carefully, then."

He laughed again. "You sound like my mother."

I had no sooner hung up the phone than it rang again. This time it was Racine.

"Ashley, did you see something again at the old house last night?" She leaped right into the subject without preliminaries. "Is somebody there?"

"Sure," I said. "Gideon's there." I knew that would throw her.

"Really? Ashley, if there's really a ghost there and you're not telling me, I'm going to fry you."

"There's no ghost, Racine."

"Well, I didn't think so. What I called about was to tell you my mom is coming home tonight, unless the baby arrives, and she wants to talk to you. Can you ride over here tomorrow morning?"

Richard wouldn't arrive until night, so I'd have plenty of time. "Sure, I guess so."

Racine cleared her throat. "How come she wants to see you, Ashley?"

"I don't know. Didn't she tell you?"

"Nobody tells me anything, except to take care of the kids."

Suddenly I felt sorry for Racine. She was one we all depended on, but we didn't tell her our secrets. She'd let my life flow freely into hers, but I'd built a dam to keep her out of mine, even though she had proved she could keep a secret.

"Listen, girl," I said, "I'll give you an earful next time I see you."

"I'll be right over."

I laughed. "How about tomorrow morning when I come to see your mother? Maybe I'll know a lot more to tell you then."

"I guess I can wait," Racine grumbled.

Mom needed my help that afternoon. Along with Finn and Truman, I weeded the garden. Funny how fast those weeds could spring up. Mom had planted flowers in between the rows of vegetables, so it was going to be very pretty eventually.

I wondered if I'd be there to see. What did Richard have in mind?

"Have you ever heard of a garden of glass flowers, Ashley?" Finn asked, and I knew the World's Greatest Authority was about to enlighten Truman and me.

"Never heard of such a thing," I said. My mind was too full of Richard and Gideon to care about anything Finn had to say. I was glad Gideon had asked me to meet him that afternoon. Maybe I could talk him into getting some help before I left with Richard.

Finn stopped weeding. He was on his knees alongside a row marked "radishes."

"There's a glass garden at Harvard University," he said. "It's the only place in the world where tropical orchids and Arizona cactus and alpine flowers can grow right next to one another."

"Really?" Truman looked at Finn in awe. He was always a fascinated audience for his older brother.

"There are 847 different kinds of glass plants." Finn was obviously going to expand on the subject.

I'd been tiptoeing around the memory of Gideon's soft, sweet kiss. Forget it, I told myself sternly. "How do you know all these things?" I asked Finn.

"I read a lot. By the time I grow up, I'll know everything in the world."

"Wow!" Truman said.

I hoped I wouldn't be around to listen to all those things Finn was going to learn. But in a way, I'd miss him. And Truman, too. I hadn't realized that before.

Oh, who needed them? Being with Richard was all that mattered.

After we finished the weeding, I told Mom I was going for a ride. Abel was up in a field, so I didn't have to answer any questions.

I hadn't been to the cemetery before, but I knew where it was. I could see it as soon as Skyrocket snailed around the point of Nelson Hill. It was on a high plot of ground across from the general store and behind the church. You got there by way of an unpaved road overhung by those ever-present cottonwood trees.

A cattle guard had been placed at the entrance to the cemetery, and Skyrocket wouldn't cross it. That spooked me at first because I thought it was the cemetery itself he didn't want to enter. But then I realized he was afraid to put his hooves on the closely spaced bars across the two-foot-deep pit. I tied him to a cottonwood tree and walked into the cemetery myself. I stood looking at the tall granite and marble headstones at the lower end. Farther up, the lawn was flat, with graves marked by low stones. That probably meant that the older graves were near where I stood.

Gideon wasn't there yet. I figured I might as well find his grave. Or the grave that for some reason he thought was his.

Veering off the roadway, I began to read the headstones. "Peter Graham, died August 4, 1880. Jens Nielsen, died September 16, 1878." Must have been early settlers. I wondered where their houses had been. Were they still there? If I were staying, I might find out. "Anne Marie Jensen, died January 6, 1910." That was close to the date of George's death. Gideon must be somewhere nearby.

Halfway up the hill I found what I was looking for. There were two white headstones, side by side: George Glessing, died July 7, 1909, and Gideon Glessing, died October 9, 1930. Gideon had probably asked to be buried beside his brother.

I was looking at the grave when suddenly Gideon spoke.

"I see you found it."

I jumped, startled. "Why do you creep up on me like that? How can you walk so silently?"

He smiled. "When I was a kid I wanted to be an Indian when I grew up. I learned how to walk without making a sound, which was how I thought they walked. Like ghosts."

"You're not a ghost," I said. "I would have known it that night on the bridge when you offered your hand, if I'd had the courage to touch it. Right?"

"I figured you wouldn't take the chance."

"So you're admitting you know you're not a ghost."

"I'm not admitting anything. I'm just answering your question."

I put my hands on my hips. "Gideon, you asked me here to this dismal place so we could talk about your problems, and now you're being slippery again."

He shook his head. "I didn't ask you here to talk about my problems. We're here to talk about yours."

He squatted down in front of the headstone that stood over Gideon Glessing's grave. Reaching over to touch the cold marble, he said, "You must change your plans, Ashley, or you might have one of these for your very own. Like me."

Chapter Eleven

Gideon's voice was ragged as he spoke. What terrible thing had happened to make him believe his body was lying beneath that stone? Did he really believe it? What could I say to him? How could I make him know that I was in no danger with Richard? Richard, who loved me and would never do anything to harm me.

Somewhere nearby a calf blatted and a cow mooed in return, a soothing, comforting sound in the gathering dusk.

I knelt beside Gideon.

"That's not you under there, Gideon," I said. "You're not a ghost. You're not Gideon Glessing."

In answer he pulled a wallet from a back pocket. Opening it, he showed me a Wyoming driver's license, bearing the name Gideon Glessing. There was a picture of him, and his birthdate, seventeen years before.

"Okay, so you *are* Gideon Glessing." Did names really make a difference, the way Racine said? Was it the name that was Gideon's problem? "But since when do ghosts have drivers' licenses?" I asked him.

He turned to look at me, his eyes glazed over with

pain. Then his face softened, the deep lines smoothing out, the muscles relaxing. He smiled, and I remembered that swift, tender kiss in the darkness the night before.

"Gideon, tell me what's wrong."

"Do you care, Ashley?"

"Of course I care." I put my hand on his arm. "I want to help."

"Why?"

Why? A few days before I hadn't even known he existed. Why should I care about his pain? But now his life had touched mine. I was involved in it.

"I want you to stop hurting," I said.

"That can never be." He leaned forward a little until his forehead rested against the cold headstone. "I'm Gideon the guilty. The hurt will never stop."

"You're Gideon the gentle," I said. "Gideon the good. Let me help you. Let Mrs. McFadden help you."

"I'm Gideon the grave." He shifted so that he was sitting with his back to the stone, his arms circling his drawn-up knees. When he looked at me, I saw that he was smiling. Teasing again. "How is she?" he asked. "Mrs. McFadden, I mean."

"She's coming home tonight. Racine said the baby isn't ready to come yet."

"Poor baby. It's a hard old world to come into." His eyes darkened. "Or go out of."

I looked out across the valley where the coming night made tall shadows up the mountainside.

"Gideon, this grave here — is it some relative? You have to be related, since you have the same name."

"Yes. He was my great-grandfather."

"So why have you been pretending to be his ghost?"

"He is me," Gideon said. "I am him." He turned his

head to smile again. "Or is that 'he is I and I am he'? English never was my best subject."

Despite the smile, he looked so sad that I took his hand and slid over next to him. He leaned his head against mine. We sat that way against the icy gravestone until Skyrocket nickered to let us know it was time to go home.

We didn't go home together, Gideon and I. He stood by the grave while Skyrocket carried me down the narrow road to the main highway. I guess he went home the same way he came, along the top of the low mountain where he could see the river on the other side. The dark, silent river that was somehow related to his pain.

Mom was worried when I got home, and Finn and Truman came to touch my hand as if to make sure I was all right.

"Where have you been?" Mom asked. "I expected you home a long time ago."

Had I been gone that long? "How come you worry about me? Isn't this supposed to be such a *safe* place?"

"You could have fallen off the horse, or something."

Finn backed away from me. "Hey, Mom, if I sassed you like she does, you'd hit me." He sounded offended.

"Don't hit her," Truman said. "I'm glad she's home. I was afraid the ghost got her."

"Ghost? What ghost?" Had something happened while I'd been gone? Had somebody found Gideon out?

"Oh, it's just something the McFadden kids told Finn and Truman." Mom rolled her eyes.

"LaVere McFadden *said*," Finn interrupted, "that Whit and the other guys saw a ghost up at the old house last night when you went up there, Ashley. They're going up again soon to see if they can catch it."

"You didn't say anything about this last night," Mom said to me. "Did something strange happen up there?"

I shrugged. "Who knows what was part of the show and what wasn't? They had this guy pretending to be the ghost, then somebody else started whamming on the house and yelling outside. Whit said it was probably some of the other guys playing a joke on all of us."

I wished I felt as calm as I sounded. I didn't know what would happen if they found Gideon. I would have to warn him again. Or maybe go up to the old house with them.

But Richard was arriving the next day.

Gideon could take care of himself, couldn't he? Besides, wasn't it about time he came back to the real world? But maybe that wasn't my decision to make.

I'd ask Mrs. McFadden about it the next day when I saw her.

I was nervous that night. I wished I knew if Richard had decided to stay in Blue Creek. Why wouldn't he tell me over the phone what it was he wanted to talk about? If he was going back to California, I ought to pack a duffel bag. I knew how restless he was. He might not want to stay in Blue Creek very long. Unless he'd decided to stay permanently.

I thought about how I'd tell Mom and Dad I really had to go back to California, if that's what Richard was going to do. Maybe they'd see how right for each other we were, if he stayed there with us for a few days. Maybe all their objections would fade away. Maybe they'd like him as much as I did.

All of Gideon's silly warnings fluttered briefly around my head like a flock of twittering birds. I shooed them away.

When I went to the McFadden house the next day, I expected to find Mrs. McFadden in bed with her feet propped up. But she was bouncing around the kitchen, ladling things into large plastic freezer containers. Racine was stacking the containers on a tray and carrying them downstairs, where I assumed they had a freezer. Kids were everywhere, sticking fingers into the containers or licking spoons.

"I'm glad you could come, Ashley." Mrs. McFadden waved a dripping ladle at me. "I'm almost through here; then I'd like to talk to you."

"I thought you'd be taking it easy." I looked around, amazed at all the activity.

Mrs. McFadden laughed. "I'd rather take it easy *after* the baby's here. So we're putting a bunch of meals in the freezer."

Racine was lifting another large tray stacked with filled containers. "She doesn't want to have to depend on my cooking." She smiled at her mother. "What is it you guys are going to talk about?"

I knew she was feeling left out again, and I was sorry I'd forgotten to ask Gideon if I could tell her about him.

Mrs. McFadden swung over to give Racine a swift peck on the cheek. "Sorry, honey, this has to be a secret between Ashley and me, for the time being."

Racine put the tray back down. "What's the matter, don't you think you can trust me? Am I going to blab everything over the party line if you let me in on the secret?"

"What secret, Mom?" asked one of the kids, whose name I think was LaVere. Or maybe that one was Delmer.

All of the kids looked our way, and soon we were surrounded by small people demanding to know secrets.

Mrs. McFadden laughed again. "I'll whisper a secret into your ears if you'll just scat for a while."

The kids lined up and got their ears whispered into, then scatted.

Mrs. McFadden whispered into Racine's ear too. I heard what she said. It was "I love you."

"Do I have to scat now too?" Racine asked. "Do I have to be one of the little kids who gets shoved out while the grownups talk? If I change my name to Florence Nightingale or somebody else noble, will you let me stay?"

I remembered my earlier thoughts that a name might make a difference. At least it seemed to make a difference to Gideon, having his great-grandfather's name.

Mrs. McFadden rested her arms across the bulk of the coming baby. "Well, Racine Wisconsin seems like a noble enough name to me. What do you think, Ashley?"

I folded my arms across my stomach in the same pose and looked at Racine. "I don't know. I've always kind of favored Duluth Minnesota."

"Stop teasing," Racine said. "I'm serious about this."

"I don't think Gideon will mind if I tell all *I* know," I said, "which isn't much."

Mrs. McFadden put down her ladle. "We'll finish this later. Let's go into the parlor where I can put my feet up." She rubbed the scar on her face, which showed up more when she was tired.

The McFadden ancestors watched from their perches on the wall while Mrs. McFadden and I told what we knew of Gideon. But I was sure Mrs. McFadden didn't tell *all* she knew.

"I wanted you to come today to bring me up to date, Ashley," she said. "Whit and Racine said there was somebody at the old house Sunday night. Was it Gideon?"

I glanced over at Racine. "Yes, it was."

"Oh, wow." Her eyes were big. "And he carried you off into the darkness, just like a romance novel."

Mrs. McFadden was shaking her head. "Oh, that foolish boy. I was hoping he'd hide out on the mountaintop while all of you kids were there at the house."

"He said he wanted to play a joke on us," I said. "He wanted to provide a little authenticity to the initiation."

"Foolish," Mrs. McFadden repeated. "But I guess he gets bored there all alone. I just don't know what would have happened if they'd seen him and gone after him. He's in such a fragile state of mind right now."

"How do you know him, Mom?" Racine asked. "How come you haven't told us about him?"

Mrs. McFadden didn't say how she knew him. All she said was, "I met him when he first came here. I've been giving him food. I put out a signal when it's safe for him to come get it. Abel Morehead knows about him too. Gideon asked us not to tell anyone else."

"Why not?" Racine sounded breathless, like a little child who can't wait to hear the next part of the story.

Mrs. McFadden leaned her head back against the sofa. "He said he has to work out his problems by himself and he'd run away if people started coming up to talk him out of it. His folks know he's there, and I keep them up to date on how he's doing. They live in Wyoming, which is where he's from. He came here because he knew the story of his great-grandfather."

"Somebody's going to find out about him soon," Racine said. "Whit and the other guys are going up to see if somebody's hiding out there. Laser says somebody made fools out of them all on Monday night, and they're out to get even. They might even go this afternoon."

I stood up. "This afternoon?"

Racine looked up at me. "It's easier to see in the day-time. Do you think we should go up there and tell him?"

"Maybe Ashley should go alone," Mrs. McFadden said. "He already knows her, and she's less likely to be seen by anybody else." She stood up and came over to me. "I wish I could go there. He needs so much help."

"For what, Mrs. McFadden? What's Gideon's problem? What's he done that makes him hide out and pretend he's a ghost?"

"Hasn't he told you?"

"No. It has something to do with having the same name as the one on the headstone in the cemetery, I think. Some-how he's involved with the past. Is that possible?"

"Yes. Oh, yes." Mrs. McFadden looked up at the faces of all those McFaddens whose pictures were on the walls. "You can't imagine how much the past can return to haunt you."

Well, well, I thought. Gideon isn't the only one who has secrets.

I urged Skyrocket into a bone-cracking trot all the way home. I had to carry my message to Gideon before Richard arrived, which could be any time. I didn't want to be up there at the old house when he drove in. Mom might turn him around and send him right back home.

The trouble was, I couldn't find Gideon.

I tied Skyrocket to a cottonwood tree and walked all around the house, calling Gideon's name. He didn't answer. Except for the murmur of the creeks in the near distance, the whole place was as quiet as a grave.

Chapter Twelve

The old house was so deserted and empty that I could almost believe again that Gideon was a ghost, even though I knew better now. But there had to be some clue, some sign that he'd been there—a sleeping bag, maybe, or food. Clothes. I'd never seen him in anything but those old-fashioned clothes that looked like something his great-grandfather must have worn.

I found nothing. I even searched in the surrounding woods and along the creek bank for a stash of some kind.

Nothing.

It gave me a sense of unreality to know that a living person occupied the premises—or *had* occupied, at least—and yet to feel nothing whatsoever of him.

"Gideon," I wailed. I was reminded of Cathy in *Wuthering Heights*, crying out across the moors for Heathcliff.

There was only the chitter of a woodchuck somewhere on the mountain.

I wondered for the hundredth time why Gideon had chosen to hide there in that lonely place. Then I chided myself. It was really none of my business why. It was his choice to be there. Wasn't that what I'd been fighting for?

The right to make my own choice? Wasn't that why I wanted to go back to California with Richard — to show that I had control over my own life?

No. No. I wanted to go back with him because I *loved* him. I wanted to be where he was. I ought to be able to make my own decisions.

In my confusion I began walking and found myself following the steep, rocky trail that led to the top of the hill. When I got there I looked down at that dark, silent river, flowing endlessly through its narrow valley on its way to the sea.

Suddenly I was frightened. Gideon had spoken at the cemetery of it being a hard world *to go out of*.

"Oh, Gideon, no," I whispered, and then I called, "Gideon! Gideon!"

The echo came back faintly. "Gideon. Gideon."

It seemed filled with despair.

Mom was annoyed with me when I got home.

"Where have you been, Ashley? You were going over to the McFaddens' for just a little while. You've been gone for hours. I need your help today. Dad called and said his assistant is ill, and he wants me to go into the office to help him for a few days."

She was spreading lasagna noodles in the bottom of a couple of flat casserole dishes. A pot of sauce bubbled on the stove, and Finn was slowly stirring it. Truman was busy grating cheese. I was reminded of the activity at the McFadden house.

"I want to get some meals done ahead of time," Mom went on. "That means you won't have to cook while I'm at Dad's office, so I'd think you'd be interested in helping."

I wondered what this whole thing would mean for

Richard and me. Would I be able to leave when Richard was ready to go? And what about Gideon? If he didn't show up before I left, could I really leave without knowing what happened to him?

"I'm sorry, Mom. I guess I'm not thinking clearly, what with Richard coming today sometime."

"Richard," Mom groaned. "Is it today he's coming?"

"Mom," I said, "just give me time to make a phone call and I'll be your right arm all afternoon."

"Richard." Mom was shaking her head. "How can I go off and leave all day when Richard's here? Why do all the bad things happen at once?"

I left her muttering to herself and went into the hallway to the telephone. My finger trembled a little as I dialed the McFaddens' number. Mom thought Richard was bad news. If only she knew what else was going on, what *really* serious things were right under her nose!

"Racine?" I said when she answered.

"Ashley? Did you find Gideon?"

"No. May I talk to your mother?"

"Secrets again?" She sounded hurt.

"No, you can listen in. Just let me talk to your mom."

I heard her yell to her mother to pick up the bedroom phone, which probably meant Mrs. McFadden was taking it easy.

There was a click, and Mrs. McFadden said, "Ashley, what's wrong?"

"Gideon's not anywhere around and I'm worried," I said. "Has he ever been suicidal, do you know?"

"No, no, I don't think so. He's been pretty depressed, but I don't think that it's ever gone that far." Mrs. Mc-Fadden sounded worried. "He's overwhelmed with guilt, but we've talked about it. Maybe he just didn't feel like seeing you today. What makes you think something's wrong?"

I could hear Racine breathing on the other phone. She listened without interrupting, and I appreciated that.

"I guess it's just that I couldn't find him. And he seemed so sad when we were at the cemetery yesterday." I pulled at a lock of hair, remembering. "He asked about you."

"He's been so interested in the baby," Mrs. McFadden said. "He says the baby is the future, and something can still be done about the future. No, Ashley, he wouldn't do away with himself. He's been shifting his view to the future, away from the past."

Not yesterday. He'd been strictly in the past yesterday. Maybe I had caused him to look backward again and give up.

"He'll show up, Ashley." Mrs. McFadden sounded concerned. "Sometimes he goes for long walks in the mountains. Try not to worry, honey."

"Ashley?" Racine's voice was tentative. "Would you like me to come over and go with you to look for him?"

"No. Thanks, Racine, but Mom's got me nailed down. I'll try to get away when those guys come to look for the ghost. Can you come then?"

"I was going to call you about that," Racine said. "Whit told me they probably won't go today since Laser is all tied up working with his dad. He thinks they'll probably go late tomorrow afternoon."

That postponed one of my worries. "Good. Maybe I'll be able to find Gideon before that. But Richard's coming tonight, and I don't know when I can get away."

"Richard!" Racine's squeal was filled with excitement. "Why didn't you tell me before? Are you going to let me meet him?" She lowered her voice. "Does he have a friend?"

"You'll get to meet him, Racine. He'll be around for a few days."

I wondered if I dared tell her I might be leaving with him. I needed to talk it over with somebody. I couldn't tell Mom and Dad yet. No use upsetting them if Richard had decided to stay in Blue Creek.

But I couldn't tell Racine with her mother on the line. She wouldn't approve of what I was planning. Mothers are all alike that way.

"Call me if you see any sign of Gideon," Mrs. Mc-Fadden said. "Right now I can't go looking for him myself."

"I'll keep thinking positively," I said. "He'll show up."

I spent the afternoon putting casseroles together for freezing and worrying about how I could talk Richard into staying until Dad's assistant got well so Mom would be back home with Finn and Truman. Or maybe I could talk Racine into coming over to stay with them after I left. She'd probably do it if I told her what was up.

But her mother could be going to the hospital any minute. She'd be needed at home.

Maybe Finn and Truman could stay over there, at the McFadden house. No, I couldn't ask that. Richard would just have to stay until Mom could be home full-time again.

But what would I do if he wouldn't?

Richard came at dusk, when the long shadows were crawling up the mountainsides like slinky cats. He came perched behind the wheel of his snappy little red pickup. He'd jacked up the springs and put on huge tires so that the truck rode several feet off the ground.

"Hey, Babe," he yelled, running across the broad lawn to where I'd been standing on the porch, watching for him. I ran too, and we must have looked like one of those TV commercials where the guy and the girl run toward each other across a flowered meadow while the music swells to a crescendo in the background. Only there was no music except for the chatter of a magpie out near the barn and the steady splash of the creek.

Who needed music? Richard was there. Richard, with that ever-present rabbit's foot bouncing from one of the belt loops on his jeans. Richard, with his hair shorter than usual, probably in an effort to look more acceptable to my parents.

He lifted me off my feet and swung me around in a hug that shut off my breath and threatened to crack some ribs. When he finally put me down and kissed me, I thought I'd die from happiness.

Richard liked Blue Creek.

"Those old hills are just waiting for my wheels," he said, flipping a thumb at the motorcycle riding in the back of his truck.

"Richard," I said breathlessly, "are you going to stay here?"

He grinned. "Well, four or five days maybe. But what I have in mind is a lot better than that."

I grabbed his arm with both hands and shook it a little. "Well, tell me what it is. I've been going crazy ever since your phone call."

His grin widened. "Let's get back in the truck for a minute."

He helped me climb up to the high seat, then got in himself. I imagined whizzing along a freeway, looking down on the tops of all the other cars.

"How do you like it?" Richard asked.

"I can't wait to take a ride in it."

"How would you like to call it home for the summer?"

I looked at him, puzzled. "What do you mean, call it home?"

He shifted around so he was facing me. "Listen, Ashley, let's get married and just take off for the rest of the summer. We can go where we want to go and do what we want to do. If we like it, we won't even go back to California."

"Wait a minute, now." I put up a hand. "You mean we'd just travel around doing nothing?"

"Doing nothing?" He bounced a little on the seat. "No, not 'doing nothing,' Ashley. Doing whatever we want to do. Nobody to order us around and tell us what to do. No parents, no schoolteachers, no Mr. Higgins and his dumb hardware store. It's all such a drag, Ashley. Let's take off."

He reached for me, but I pulled back.

"Richard, I couldn't do that. My parents would never let me go off like that."

He laughed. "Well then, don't tell them, idiot-girl. We'll just leave in the middle of the night. We can find a justice of the peace somewhere who'll marry us."

I stared at him.

"It's *our* lives, Ashley," he said softly. "Let's live them the way *we* want."

"Richard, no, I don't think I can do it that way. I just figured maybe you could stay here, or I could go back to California with you and we'd finish school and then we'd be old enough to do what we want."

"Why wait?" He pointed to the back of his truck. "I've got a couple of sleeping bags back there and a big box of grub." Opening the glove compartment, he took out the big pistol he'd taught me how to shoot. "I even brought my protector. There's nothing to worry about. It'll be a blast, Ashley."

To show what a "blast" it would be, he put his arm with the pistol out of the window, aimed at a tree, and said, "Blam!"

Dad drove into the yard just then. He spotted the pistol right away. Stopping the car, he got out and came over to Richard's truck, looking up at us.

"Hello, Richard," he said. "I hope that gun isn't loaded."

"It isn't, sir," Richard said politely. "I'd never carry a loaded gun."

"I'll have to ask you to lock it up while you're here," Dad went on. "No target practicing. Finn and Truman could be just about anywhere, to say nothing of the farm animals."

"Dad," I said, "he was just showing it to me. He wasn't going to shoot it." I leaned across Richard to look down at Dad.

He nodded. "Okay. I'm just establishing some guidelines." He cleared his throat. "How are you, Richard?"

"Fine, sir. I really like your place here." Richard put the gun back into the glove compartment and locked it.

Dad relaxed a little. "Thanks. We like it, too." He turned to go. "Mom will be expecting you in for dinner shortly."

"We'll be right in," I assured him.

As soon as he was gone, Richard turned to me again. "Well, what do you say? Are we going to take off for a terrific summer?"

I can't say I wasn't tempted. But it just wasn't the kind of thing I could do. Even for Richard.

"I'm sorry," I said, shaking my head. "Richard, why can't you just stay here? You said you like it."

"Not that much," Richard said. "Think about it, Ashley. Maybe you'll change your mind."

I didn't think so. But I couldn't let Richard go off without me, either.

The next morning we got a big lecture from both Mom and Dad before they left for Prentiss. They gave us endless instructions about what we could and couldn't do, and how we had to watch Finn and Truman. And no guns.

They left eventually, Mom with a worried look on her face and Dad telling Finn and Truman to be good.

As soon as they were out of sight, Richard said, "All *right!* Let's live a little. Who wants a motorcycle ride?"

"Me," Finn yelled, and Truman echoed, "Me."

"No." I put both hands up, palms out. "No way."

"Okay." Richard was agreeable. "What can we do?"

"We could go find the ghost," Finn said. He told Richard about how the older guys were going on a ghost hunt.

"That's not until later," I said. I didn't want Richard to have to confess that he was superstitious and probably wouldn't go near the old house under any circumstances. "What else would you like to do, guys?"

"Innertubing on the river," Truman sang out.

"Sounds like something worth trying," Richard said. "What do you say, Ashley?"

I was full of objections. Mom wouldn't approve. There were bad currents in the river. People had drowned there.

"Your folks didn't include that on the list of things you were forbidden to do," Richard said. "Look, what's the big deal? I've been a lifeguard at the community pool, and I've surfed and swum in the ocean."

How could I confess that my biggest worry was seeing Gideon floating sodden and dead just under the surface of that smooth river?

I gave in.

We borrowed innertubes and soon were bouncing along the rough, narrow road that led down to the river. Richard drove too fast for a road he didn't know. But he was a good driver, and we got there safely.

Finn and Truman could hardly wait to get into the water, but I made them wait until I dispensed what knowledge I had about innertubing. I don't think they listened, but at least they waited.

Finally we all got aboard our innertubes and let the current take us.

"Last one out in the middle's a chicken," said Richard, paddling furiously with his hands.

Finn and Truman followed his example.

The words made me uneasy, and I soon realized why. Richard was giving the boys a dare, and it had been a dare that had caused the drowning all those years ago when Gideon had dared his brother to swim across this same river.

It wasn't until I saw Truman spinning wildly in tight little circles that I remembered something else. The dam! They must be letting water through the dam that day, which made swifter currents than usual. We should have checked about the dam before we came!

"Richard," I screamed, "the current. It's bad."

He laughed across the water. "Don't be such a worry-wart, Ashley. It's great!"

But as Truman was suddenly swept downstream, even Richard got nervous.

"Paddle, Truman," he yelled. "Paddle to the bank."

Truman was enjoying his adventure. He must have thought this was what innertubing was all about.

"I don't want to," he yelled back.

He was getting too far away. Richard tried to paddle into the same current, but another one caught him and swirled him toward the opposite bank.

"Come on, you guys," Truman yelled, his voice faint and far away now.

I began to pray. "Oh, please, don't let him get scared and try to get out of the tube."

Finn was watching from a relatively calm spot near me. "I think I'll get out," he said, paddling to the bank.

"Richard," I screamed, pointing frantically at Truman.

Richard gave up on the innertube. Flipping out of it, he swam swiftly toward the center of the river, letting the current snatch him and sweep him toward Truman. It didn't take him long to catch up, but the trouble wasn't over. He couldn't get either himself or Truman out of that current. What would happen if they drifted as far as the dam?

I struggled to the bank with some idea of jumping into Richard's truck and driving down to the dam. Maybe somebody could stop the outlet of water. Maybe I could somehow fish Richard and Truman out.

I was dashing for the truck when Finn yelled, "They're out!"

Looking back, I saw Richard swimming strongly, tugging Truman and his innertube toward shore.

"Oh, Richard, thank you," I whispered, turning back to the truck to get the towels we'd brought.

That's when I saw Gideon running down the hill. His jacket was off and he was just dropping his shirt. He'd been preparing to go into the water to save Truman and

Richard. He stopped when he saw they were out, and before any of the others saw him, he disappeared once again into the trees.

My relief at seeing him again was threaded with worry. What effect would this near reenactment of the long-ago drowning have on him? And what connection did it have to his own problem?

Chapter Thirteen

Truman talked about his adventure all the way home. "That old water whirled me like crazy," he said. "I really like innertubing. It's better than the log ride at Magic Mountain."

That's all it was to him—just another ride, in another big playland. No danger involved. No harm done, since Richard had been there to rescue him.

But it had been Richard's idea to go to the river in the first place. If he hadn't come, the whole thing wouldn't have happened.

On the other hand, we wouldn't have gone into the water if I'd remembered to check with the people in charge of the power station to see if they were letting water through the dam that day.

And if I'd just plain said no, I could have stopped the whole thing.

Finn was quiet. Just before we got home, he said, "Are we going to tell Mom and Dad about this?"

"No sense in worrying them," Richard said before I could speak. "Everything turned out just fine, didn't it?"

"Ashley?" Finn said.

What could I say? If I said yes, we should tell them, I'd be contradicting Richard.

If I said no, we shouldn't tell them, what would that be teaching Finn?

"What do *you* think?" I said.

"I don't know," Finn said. "That's why I asked you."

It was too late to make explanations, because we drove into our yard and saw Whit's battered blue van parked there. Whit and Racine and a bunch of guys were standing around it.

I hadn't expected they'd be going up to the old house that early. How would I warn Gideon now?

But why did I need to? He'd been watching at the river. He was probably watching us now, aware of what was going on. That must have been how he'd known my name, my plans. He'd overheard me talking to Abel. He'd been nearby when Mom had yelled out what she'd needed from the store that day I met him. That was how he'd known all those things. There was a perfectly logical explanation for it.

"Hey," Laser called as we came to a stop, "we were just about to leave. You almost missed the Great Ghost Hunt."

Richard stopped with one foot out of the truck. "Ghost hunt?"

"Can Truman and I go, too, Ashley?" Finn asked.

"Oh, please," Truman begged.

"Now look, guys. I don't even know if *I'm* going." If I didn't go, then Richard would have an excuse not to go, if he was nervous about it. "Besides, haven't you had enough excitement for one day?"

"No," Finn and Truman wailed together. "We want to go!"

"Hush," I said. "Let's go over and talk about it."

We all got out of the truck and walked over to where the others were. I introduced Richard and told him the names of the guys I remembered.

Racine signaled with her eyebrows that Richard was at least a 10, but Whit scowled as he looked at me. What was the matter with him? I'd told him I had a guy in California. And there certainly hadn't been anything between Whit and me. But I guess Richard in person brought back hurtful memories from the previous summer.

"We thought you might like to go with us," Whit said through stiff lips. "But maybe you had something else in mind."

"Well," I said, "I ought to stay here with Finn and Truman."

I saw Racine nod slightly. I wasn't sure what she meant.

"What about you, Richard? Want to join us?" Laser was being friendly even though Whit wasn't.

"Fill me in on it," Richard said, and I knew he was buying a little time to think about it.

So they told him the whole story, each one putting in a few words, and the story got bigger and bigger as each one embellished it. By the time they finished, it sounded as if Gideon had been a real threat.

Richard relaxed. "Doesn't sound like a ghost. Sounds like some nut holed up there in the hills."

Whit's scowl plowed even deeper furrows in his forehead, and Laser said, "Could be. Whatever he is, we're going to find him. We don't like the idea of some goofball hanging around up there. Coming?"

"Sure. Let me change out of my swimsuit and pick up my ghostbuster. I'll be right with you." Richard headed for the house, followed by Finn and Truman.

"We're going too," Finn said, and Truman quickly echoed him.

"They can't go," I told Racine and the guys who stood around waiting. "I'll have to stay here with them." I rolled my eyes to let Racine know she had to take care of Gideon.

To my surprise, she said, "I'll stay too. It might take two of us to keep those kids here." She took my arm. "Let's go break the news to them."

We walked toward the house, and as soon as we were out of hearing distance, she said, "We'll wait until they leave, then we'll go up there too."

I looked at her. "How?"

She nodded her head toward the barn. "When we drove in, I saw Abel's old farm wagon there by the corral, with the horses already hitched to it. I expect he's gone home to lunch. There's another way to get to the house. A lot shorter, but a car couldn't make it. Horses can."

"Do you think we need to?" I asked. "Gideon will probably see them coming. Besides, they're nice guys. They wouldn't hurt him, would they?"

"I don't know, Ashley. They're in a mean mood. They think he made monkeys of them the other night, and they're out for revenge. And even if they don't hurt him physically, you know what Mom said about his mental state."

"I'll hurry and change," I said.

It wasn't easy to convince Finn and Truman to stay with us. They grumbled and whined and said they didn't want to stay there with a couple of girls when all the guys were going after a ghost.

But as soon as the guys left, we told them we were taking a wagon ride, and suddenly they were happy again.

I wished they could stay home, but I couldn't leave them alone and I didn't know when Abel would be back.

I just hoped he didn't mind our using his wagon.

The trail where Racine guided the horses was rough and rutted and narrow. She urged them along as fast as they could go, and we all jounced and bounced around in the wagon box. Finn and Truman thought it was wonderful. They didn't question why we were traveling this way when we could have gone in the van with the guys. This was more fun.

"We'll get there before the guys do," Racine whispered to me. "They have that long hike. This trail will take us to the top of the hill. We can each take a different direction heading down toward the house, and one of us will find Gideon."

"What about the boys?" I whispered.

Racine guided the horses around a fallen tree trunk, then said, "We'd better have them stay with the wagon. They'll be safer there than where the action is."

I worried about that. But when we got to the top of the hill, Racine tied the horses firmly to a tree and it seemed safe enough.

"Listen, guys," I told them. "This is important. We need somebody to stay here in the wagon and make sure the horses stay put. Do you think you can do that?"

"No," Finn said, "I want to see the ghost."

Racine and I gave them a snow job about how important it was to take care of the horses and make sure they were ready for a quick get-away, if necessary. Finn and Truman grumbled, but they agreed to stay—if we'd bring the ghost back up there when we caught it.

Down in the valley we could see Whit and Richard and the other guys toiling up the trail that ran alongside the creek. We'd have to hurry if we were going to scout the mountainside all the way down to the house, then get out of sight again.

"Let's go," Racine said. "You go to the right and I'll take the left. Call Gideon, but not too loud. We don't want the guys to hear."

With a backward glance at Finn and Truman, who watched me with big, trusting eyes, I started down the hill. I hadn't ever thought much before about what effect I had on them. They led their lives and I led mine. But the fact was that our lives were intertwined and tangled together. The way Gideon said.

I walked as quietly as I could, calling softly for Gideon. Maybe he had stayed down by the river. Laser and the others would never find him there. But what if he'd come back to wherever he had his stash of food to eat? Perhaps he fell asleep afterward. What if he awakened to see all those big guys surrounding him?

"Gideon," I called.

I heard soft rustles in the woods nearby, almost like somebody walking, but Gideon didn't appear. It must have been a small animal.

When I came to another point where I could see the guys, I saw they were in a circle, talking. After a short consultation, they broke into four sets of two, each set taking a different approach to the old house. Richard and Whit continued up the main path. They would probably arrive first.

I speeded up, zigzagging down through the trees, whispering Gideon's name.

I was almost to the old house when I found him. He was standing by a tree, listening, every muscle alert.

"Gideon," I said.

"Shh." He put a finger to his lips. "They're coming."

He turned wild eyes toward me.

"It's Whit," I said. "And Laser. And Richard and some others."

He shook his head. "No. It's *them*. They're coming for me. They hate me."

I took his arm. "Come on. Let's go back up the hill. Racine and I have horses and a wagon there. We'll get away."

He shook his head again. "Two of them are circling up that way. They're surrounding me."

I heard voices nearby.

"We'll go at the house from the back," one of them said. "There's an old cellar back there that I'll bet nobody'll think to look in."

"That's where my stuff is," Gideon whispered. "I didn't think anybody knew about that cellar."

"So that's why I couldn't find any trace of you when I came to tell you about these guys coming."

He looked at me, and his eyes cleared a little. "Why are you doing all this for me, Ashley?"

"I like you, Gideon. I want to help. I told you that."

He took in a deep breath, then let it out in a long sigh. "Thank you for trying," he said.

I pulled at his arm again. "Let's go up the hill now. We can get away."

But it was too late. There was the crack of a branch nearby, and some loud rustling.

"Who's there?" someone called.

Whit and Richard came around the corner of the old house. Richard's eyes darted nervously, searching the bushes. Whit walked stiffly. Angrily. "Keep that thing in your pocket," he said.

"Look, man, I know what I'm doing." Richard's hand hovered near his pocket.

And suddenly I knew what he'd meant by his "ghost-buster." He had that ugly pistol with him. Talking about ghosts had always made him nervous, so he'd put his courage into his pocket.

"Gideon," I rasped, "we've *got* to get out of here."

"Hey, I found something!" That was Laser's voice. "There's grub in the old cellar. And a sleeping bag."

"So it *is* a guy," Whit said. "Probably some crazy who's hiding out from the police."

Gideon seemed paralyzed. I couldn't yank him away from his post by the tree.

All of the guys came running from wherever they'd been. Then everything happened at once.

There was another loud crack and more rustling. Richard whirled around, whipping the pistol from his pocket and aiming it at the source of the noise. Right at Truman, who came scampering out of the bushes.

"No!" yelled Gideon, plunging into the clearing and running toward Richard, who was still holding that big ugly cannon.

Richard stepped back, shifting the pistol to aim at Gideon. It seemed like slow motion as Whit moved forward to grab at Richard's arm, and the pistol swung down, down, and went off.

Everybody froze. Gideon was in a half crouch. Whit and Richard and Laser and the others stared at him, then down at Whit's boot, from which blood was beginning to ooze. Then back at Gideon.

"Who's he?" Laser whispered hoarsely.

"It's Gideon," I said. "He's not a ghost. Let him alone."

"Ashley," Truman wailed. "Finn fell out of a tree." He

didn't even seem to see the pistol and the tense scene in front of him.

Finn appeared from the bushes, rubbing his head. "Who's got firecrackers? I heard one go off."

I snatched at his arm. "Bawl," I said. "Bawl *loud*."

"I'm too big to bawl," Finn said. "I didn't get hurt."

"Bawl anyway. Say your arm is broken. *BAWL!*"

Finn bawled.

His cries cut through the silence. Racine burst into the clearing. "Who got shot?" She rushed up to Finn. "Finn! Finn, are you all right?"

Finn bellowed. "My arm's busted," he said.

The attention shifted to him. But Gideon was still crouched, his eyes wild again. Richard still held the gun. Whit's foot still bled. Laser was poised to attack but didn't seem to know who to go after.

The others watched Finn.

I ran to Gideon.

"Gideon." I shook his shoulder. "We have to get Whit to the hospital. Do you have anything we can wrap around his foot?"

Gideon looked at me blankly.

"Richard," I ordered, "get rid of that gun. And don't ever let me see it again."

Obediently, Richard put the ugly thing into his pocket.

The other guys came out of their trances. Whit sat down suddenly and began to remove his boot. Racine realized then what had happened and dashed to Whit.

"Don't take it off," she said. "That might make it bleed worse. Let's just get you to the hospital."

Finn and Truman came over to see what was happening.

"Can I stop bawling now?" Finn whispered.

"You're going to bawl a lot louder when I find out why you didn't stay where I told you," I hissed.

"I didn't think you'd find out," Finn said.

He'd had a good lesson in furtiveness from me that morning. The fault was mine. But I couldn't deal with that now. Whit needed help. I had to get Gideon moving.

"Bandages," I said to Gideon. "We need something to stuff into Whit's boot. You must have something that will do."

He didn't move.

"Whit's going to bleed to death if we don't do something," I said in a low voice so just Gideon could hear me.

That got to him. Rising slowly from that catatonic crouch, he said, "I've got towels."

I don't know who got everybody organized. Maybe it was Richard. It could even have been Gideon. I don't know. But some of the guys hauled Whit down to his van while I trotted alongside, muttering some kind of explanation about who Gideon was and why he was there.

A couple of guys, who admitted they couldn't stand the sight of blood, went up the hill to take the horses and wagon back to Abel. Finn and Truman went with them.

Gideon was functioning by the time we got to the van. He knew a lot about first aid.

"Lay him on his back," he instructed. "Elevate his foot. I'll sit by him and apply pressure."

Nobody questioned his authority.

"I'll drive, " Laser offered.

Richard was as pale as Whit. He was limp and silent except for periodically saying, "I'm sorry about the gun." All of the macho that had kept him starched was gone.

But it was Gideon I worried about.

"It's all my fault," he whispered as I sat down beside him in the back of the van. There was such a look of hopelessness on his face that I figured Racine's theory of the recycling past must be true. Was Gideon doomed to cause sorrow to other people, like his great-grandfather?

And what pattern was I setting up for myself?

Chapter Fourteen

Whit was pale by the time we got to the hospital in Prentiss, but no paler than Gideon. Or Richard, either. All of them were spattered with Whit's blood. I wondered which needed attention first.

Laser whipped the van into the emergency entrance of the small, one-story brick hospital. I was relieved to see a man in white pants and a short-sleeved white jacket come out, pushing a gurney.

"There's a doctor," I said. I'd been thinking that maybe in a small place like Prentiss, the one or two doctors would be out on other calls or maybe they'd gone fishing, and no one would be there. Whit would bleed to death, and Richard would collapse with remorse, and Gideon — what would happen to Gideon?

Racine looked out at the man in white. "That's just Ralph Cooney. He's kind of a nurse's aide. He provides the muscle power."

But Ralph seemed to know what he was doing. After a couple of terse questions, he got Richard to help him lift Whit onto the gurney while Gideon kept his pressurehold on that bloody foot.

A nurse came running down the corridor and stopped beside the gurney.

"Whit!" she said. "What's going on? Is this McFadden Day here at the hospital?" Briskly she began examining Whit's foot, still encased in the boot.

Racine put a hand to her throat, and Whit raised himself on a shaky elbow. "What do you mean?"

"Well," the nurse said, "your folks arrived almost an hour ago and your new brother put in an appearance five minutes after that. Now here *you* are."

Whit lay down again. "Oh boy. We were supposed to hang around to take care of the kids in case the baby decided it was his birthday."

Racine seemed dumfounded. "Brother? Are you sure? It was supposed to be a sister. The pattern was all set up for a girl."

"Oh?" The nurse motioned for Ralph to push Whit into a nearby room. "Then you'd better nab the stork and tell him he dropped the wrong bundle."

We followed her to the door of the room, which was filled with metal tables and shelves of gleaming instruments and rolls of bandages. This was a room dedicated to hanging onto whatever life was left in the bodies brought here. But what could it offer injured minds?

Gideon let go of Whit's boot and hung onto the door frame. "Is he all right?" he asked softly.

"Sure he is." The nurse patted Whit on the shoulder. "He's lost some blood, but he can spare it."

"No." Gideon seemed ready to slide to the floor. "The *baby*. Is *he* all right?"

"Right as rain. Big guy. Over nine pounds. Stick around for a while and he's likely to come strolling down the hallway." The nurse picked up some scissors and began cutting away the leg of Whit's jeans. "Now, all of you scoot. The doctor will be here soon, and we have work to do."

Racine stood her ground. "How bad is it?" She motioned toward Whit's foot.

The nurse continued working. "Can't tell yet. But I'd say it could have been a lot worse."

Ralph pushed us all out and closed the door.

"I have to report a gunshot wound, you know," he said to no one in particular. He went off down the hall.

Richard sat on a nearby chair, putting his head down between his knees. Poor Richard. He hadn't meant to shoot anybody. The old house and the talk of ghosts had made him nervous. I started toward him but saw Gideon trembling. "Gideon?" I said.

He looked at me, and the sweetness of his smile transformed that sterile-white corridor.

"The baby's all right," he said.

If he hadn't been, would Gideon have taken that guilt upon himself, too? I tried to think the way he did. Since Whit and Racine had been out pursuing him instead of taking care of their duties at home, he would assume it was his fault if something had gone wrong with the baby.

Oh, Gideon, Gideon, I said silently, *how can I help you?*

The doctor came then. He paused briefly alongside Gideon.

"You look green, son," he said. "The men's room is over there." He pointed down the hallway, then hurried into the emergency room and closed the door.

Gideon wobbled down the hall and disappeared inside the men's room. I thought about following him so I could help him, but I was shy about going in there. Laser had gone outside, and Richard was in no shape to help anybody.

Mr. McFadden came half-running down the hall. "Where's Whit?"

Racine pointed toward the emergency room. Mr. McFadden ran to the door, and stuck his head inside.

"How is he, Doc?" he asked.

"He'll live," the doctor called. "As soon as I plow a piece of boot out of his foot and do a little embroidery, he can go home. Go tell your wife I don't want to see another McFadden in here for the next ten years."

Mr. McFadden closed the door and came over to Racine and me. "How come you and Whit faded away just when we needed you?" he said to Racine. "We had to wait for Aunt Allie to come stay with the kids. The baby almost arrived out there on the highway." He ran his fingers through his hair. "How'd Whit manage to get himself shot?"

Racine told him quickly what had happened, then said, "How's Mom?"

"Fine. How come you weren't there when she needed you?"

Racine looked at her feet and whispered, "I'm sorry, Daddy."

Mr. McFadden took a deep breath as if he were going to blast her. But then he let it all out and smiled. "What the heck, after all the kids we've had we could have managed, even out on the highway. Mom wants to see you, Racine. And you too, Ashley. She has something she wants to talk to you about."

"I have to see Richard first," I said.

But just then a big man in a brown uniform came down the hall and stopped by Richard's chair.

"You the guy who's been shooting things up?" he asked.

"Yeah." Richard didn't raise his head.

The cop put a booted foot on the chair rung, flipped open a pad, and licked the lead of his pencil. "Wanta tell me about it?"

"Officer Thatcher must be having a slow day," Mr. McFadden said. "I'll talk to him. You girls go tell Mom Whit's okay."

I took another step toward Richard, but Mr. McFadden steered me the other way.

As Racine and I passed the men's room, we could hear Gideon throwing up.

Mrs. McFadden was sitting up when we got to her room. She looked anxious, but otherwise she was fine. Racine quickly reassured her about Whit, then filled her in on the details of the accident.

"How's Gideon?" Mrs. McFadden asked.

I shook my head. "Not good. But he did a great job of first aid on Whit."

"Oh dear, oh dear," Mrs. McFadden worried, almost under her breath. "I'm afraid this is going to bring it all back. He's going to be reliving the past again."

"That's about all he's been doing since I met him," I said. "He wears the past the way he wears those old clothes of his."

"Those were his great-grandfather's clothes," Mrs. McFadden said. "The first Gideon. He kept them as a reminder of the terrible thing he'd done, and the family hung onto them when he was gone. Gideon took them over when he . . ." She stopped.

"When he what?" I asked. "What happened to him?"

She rubbed her forehead. "That's something he has to tell you when he's ready, Ashley. He had a dreadful experience, and he saw it as part of a pattern set by his great-grandfather, then his father." She stopped again and seemed to be gazing into the past.

Racine watched with big eyes. "Did you know Gideon's father?"

Mrs. McFadden nodded slowly. "Oh, yes. Walter and I went together for a long time. His family used to come here a lot. They've always been sort of hung up on the old story of the first Gideon." She paused.

"So what happened?" Racine prompted.

"Walter was high spirited and quite rebellious," Mrs. McFadden said. "His folks tried so hard to hold him down, always warning him about what happened to his grandfather. He got involved in things he shouldn't have been into, and one night . . ." Mrs. McFadden paused again and sighed. "Remember the terrible accident I've told you about? The one where I got this scar?" She touched the scar on her face. "Walter—Gideon's father—caused that accident. He never came back here afterward because he couldn't bear to see what he'd done to me. But Gideon came to me when he first arrived in Blue Creek. He wanted to reassure himself that I was all right. It seemed important to him."

"What happened to Walter?" Racine asked. "Did he 'sorrow away' the way the first Gideon did?"

Mrs. McFadden shook her head. "No. He shaped up into a very fine man, but he's carried a bigger scar than I have all these years. I guess that's why he's letting Gideon see if he can work out his problems the way he's chosen. He understands how it is to deal with something you can't undo."

"Mrs. McFadden," I said, "who is Robbie? Can you tell me that much? Maybe Robbie could help him."

"She's dead," Mrs. McFadden said bluntly. "She was Gideon's sweetheart." She suddenly looked very tired.

"It's time you rested." Racine pressed the button that lowered her mother's bed, then tucked the sheet around her as if she were the child and Racine the mother. "I'm sorry I wasn't there today when you needed me."

Mrs. McFadden reached out a hand. "You've always been there before, Racine. Maybe we learned to appreciate you today when you weren't." She closed her eyes. "Give Whit my love. And Ashley—take care of Gideon."

Racine was the only one who said much of anything on the way home. She chattered nonstop.

When Richard and Gideon and I got out of the van at our place, I said, "I'll call you later to find out how Whit is, Racine."

"Okay," she said. "But call me LeeAnne now."

I understood. Someone had finally recognized all she'd done for so many years, and it was okay to be LeeAnne.

But what about Gideon? Was it okay to be Gideon?

And what about me?

I wondered about that again when Richard asked me to go out to his truck to talk. That was after we'd told Mom and Dad everything we knew about the day.

After Mom had tried to coax Gideon to stay the night.

After Gideon had said he had to go back to the old house.

After he went.

Finn and Truman wanted to go out to the truck with us, but when I said Richard and I were just going to talk, they lost interest. The World's Greatest Authority told me it was easy to talk but hard to say anything important.

I surprised Finn by hugging him. "You're right," I said. Then I hugged Truman too, and he hugged me back. I hadn't hugged my brothers since they were babies. But I guess you don't realize how much you love people until you see how easy it could be to lose them.

"Ashley," Richard said as soon as we were seated in the high cab of the truck. "Ashley, I'm going to split. Come with me. Let's get out of here right now." He put the key into the ignition and started the engine.

I couldn't believe what he was saying. "Right now? Just like that? Without saying anything to my folks? Without waiting to see how Whit gets along? Or Gideon?"

Richard shifted nervously on the seat. "They'll get along all right. This has been a mighty heavy day and I want to get out of here. We have our own lives to live."

Echoes of my own words. "Isn't there some legal reason why you have to stay?"

"It was an accident, Ashley. Whit's dad told the cop he's not pressing charges or anything." Richard stepped on the gas pedal, racing the engine. "Let's go. We can go back to California or whatever you want, but let's just get out of here."

I reached over to turn off the motor. "Richard, you *shot* somebody today. And it could have been a whole lot worse. What about Finn and Truman? You came close to shooting them."

Richard nodded his head slowly. "Yeah." He turned to face me. "I told that cop it was all their fault. If they hadn't come crashing out of the bushes, none of this would have happened. You should do something about those kids."

I stared at my handsome, exciting Richard while the future played through my mind like the fast scan on a

Lael Littke

VCR. I saw the past and present and future all linked together by the decisions we make.

I took Richard's hand. I felt so much older than he was.

"Richard," I said, "I have something important to tell you."

The next morning I saddled Skyrocket and rode up to the old house before it was fully light.

"Gideon," I called.

The old house was bleak in that early light of dawn.

"Gideon," I repeated.

He came, then, from somewhere inside.

"Ashley," he said, "what are you doing here?" He still wore those old clothes, now blood-spattered. He'd tried to clean them off, but the stains remained.

"I came to talk to you."

He looked at me for a moment before he said, "I don't have anything to talk about."

I went on as if he hadn't spoken. "Why don't you change out of those clothes first? Then we'll walk to the top of the hill and watch the sun rise while we talk."

He looked down at himself, touching the blood stains with his fingers.

"Robbie," he said softly.

"No. That's Whit's blood."

I don't know if he heard.

"I wear these clothes as a reminder that the pattern is set. I can't escape." He looked as desolate as the old house.

I took his hand and we started up the hill. Behind us Skyrocket nipped off the dew-wet grass and chewed contentedly, there under the cottonwood where I'd tied him.

We climbed silently for a few minutes, then Gideon said, "She was so beautiful."

"Who?" I turned to him and saw his eyes gazing into the past, the way Mrs. McFadden's had done.

"Robbie. I loved her so much. She trusted me. She thought I could handle it."

"Handle what, Gideon?" We continued to climb, slowly. I didn't want to interrupt his telling.

"The car. I said I could handle it on that steep road. Oh, no. No. No. The blood."

He let go of my hand and ran the rest of the way to the top of the hill.

I ran too, my heart bursting, my breath coming in gasps.

"Gideon," I said, "talk about Robbie. Tell me about her."

"I didn't learn," Gideon said. "Not from my great-grandfather and not from my father. I didn't think about what could happen. It's a pattern. I can't leave here. I'd just hurt somebody again."

"Gideon," I said, "you *saved* somebody yesterday. You broke the pattern."

He shook his head violently. "No. Whit would have lived no matter what *I* did." He turned to run.

I grabbed his hand again. "I'm not talking about Whit. I mean *me*, Gideon. You saved *me* from trashing my future."

He looked at me, puzzled, the tension in his body diminishing a little.

"I sent Richard away, Gideon."

"Because of the gun?"

"Not entirely. That was terribly foolish, but I could have forgiven him for that. I sent him away because of the things you told me. About the creeks, and the way our lives flow together. How everything we do affects somebody else. Some people take responsibility for the things they do. Others don't. I almost threw my life away on somebody I could never be happy with. But I didn't, Gideon, because of what you told me."

I paused for breath.

Gideon gazed at me for a long time. Then he said, "He was a lot like me. I knew that when I heard you describing him to Abel."

"Maybe the way you used to be," I said. "But you're not like that anymore. You're Gideon, the gentle. Gideon, the good. Remember?"

He gave me another of those smiles that broke my heart. "Let's talk, Ashley. I'll tell you about Robbie."

He turned to look down at the river as he spoke. It wasn't a pretty story he told.

"Robbie was my girl from the time we were in the fifth grade," he said. "She was always urging me to be more than I thought I could be. She believed in me. She believed too much in me."

"Too much?"

He nodded. "I was wild and reckless. I liked fast cars and excitement and danger. You know how when you're young you think nothing can happen to you."

He sounded as if he were a thousand years old.

"I had a pretty little VW that I'd rigged for speed. I took Robbie along on a test drive. I thought I could handle it. Robbie thought I could too."

He put his hands over his face.

"The car rolled. We landed upside down in the canal. I got out, but I couldn't get to Robbie in time. Oh, the blood. The blood." He lowered his hands and scrubbed at the stains on his clothes.

"Gideon," I said. "You don't need to say any more."

I shouldn't have made him talk. He was going to flip out again.

He drew a deep, shuddering breath. "I *want* to tell you, Ashley. Just give me a minute."

He took several deep breaths while I waited. Then he said, "There was no way I could face what I did. I came to Blue Creek to spend the rest of my life where my great-grandfather spent his. I'm so much like him. I even have his name."

"But you're *not* him, Gideon," I said.

He nodded. "I know. Sometimes I tried to convince myself that I was. If I were him—his ghost—then I could get away from my own guilt for a while. Sometimes I thought he'd come back to possess me and that he caused me to do what I did."

"Do you still think that?"

He gazed at the river. "I don't know. I wish I could believe it. Then I wouldn't have to be me."

"Gideon, you can get help with this. You don't have to carry it all alone. And haven't you heard of forgiveness?"

He was silent.

"Gideon, you have a life to live. And I do, too, because of you."

His eyes seemed to look inward, and for a scary moment I thought he was spacing out. But then he smiled at me and led me to the big flat rock there on the top of the hill. We sat down on it together and watched the morning sun paint the river pink far below us.

Gideon will be coming back soon. It's been two years since he went back to his family to get the love and professional help he needed.

"I found out that Robbie's parents forgave me a long time

ago," he wrote in his last letter, "and finally I've been able to
forgive myself. I'll never forget what I did, but I can go on with
my life now."

As a P.S. he added, "I burned those old clothes that belonged
to my great-grandfather."

I've changed a lot too. Funny how much you can see when
you open yourself up. I love Blue Creek now. LeeAnne and I
have had some wonderful, funny times together, and we'll soon
be college roommates. I've gone out with Whit a few times, but
he's like a nice big brother.

And on June 27, exactly two years from the day I first saw
Gideon, he's coming back. I don't know what's in the future. But
I do know we'll be very careful of the decisions we make when
we talk together in the shadow of the old house, up there where
the creeks meet.